CROSS ROADS

LAUREL HIGHTOWER

CROSSROADS

Laurel Hightower

OFF LIMITS PRESS

For Sebastian, because everything I have belongs to you.

CHAPTER ONE

The first time Chris buried a part of herself by her son's roadside cross, it was an accident. A cut, deep and oozing for much of the day, broken open again as she cleared fallen leaves and highway detritus from the base of the cross. She'd had an accident with a box cutter early in the morning before anyone else was at the office. It had bled like anything, and now it was doing it again. Thick drops leached into the dry earth before she noticed—it was the striking red against that painted white wood that drew her attention.

"Damn." She put the dirty finger in her mouth, sucked away the blood, and watched the dark spots in the soil recede. It had been a dry September, and the ground drew her blood deep.

"Gross, Mom. You really think that's sanitary? You used to tell me I'd get worms if I sucked my fingers after playing in the dirt."

The voice came from over her left shoulder, where it always was—where *he* always was, but she wasn't going to look. That wasn't part of the game. Instead she pictured him, the way his mouth would curve on one side only, his hair, long on top, sliding over one eye as he dug his hands into the pockets of his too-big jeans.

She smiled, knowing he wouldn't be able to see it, bent over as she was. She spat onto a tissue and worked at scrubbing the smear of blood from the cross. "I'm too mean. Worms don't want any of this."

A groan from Trey. "Ugh, that brings back memories. Here, your face has a smudge on it, let me scrub my saliva into it."

She took a final swipe and tucked the wadded tissue into her pocket. "Mother spit has magical properties, brat, and you know it."

"Cures all ills. I remember."

"Not quite all," she said in a soft voice, one hand on his cross.

A rude noise from over her left shoulder. "What have I said, Mom?"

She flicked away the single tear that had snuck down her cheek, replacing it with another smile. "I know, I know. There's no crying in baseball." She settled back, her legs folded, hands braced behind her.

"My grave, my rules."

"They were always your rules."

Though it wasn't his grave, not really. He was buried at Elmwood, near Chris's father. At first, she'd gone to visit him there because she felt like she was supposed to, despite how much it scared her. But this cross, here in the hollow where her only son's life had ended, this felt closer to him.

She hadn't known what she'd set in motion that night, leaving her unintentional blood offering, but it wouldn't have mattered. Like most evenings, she'd stayed until the sun was nearly down, the too-bright final rays piercing the shadows of the overhanging trees. She talked to Trey, catching him up on what had happened at work and smiling when her update on the recurring adventures of the bathroom bandit made him do that snort laugh she'd always loved. Passing traffic was a distant hum, dropping in frequency as it got later. Coming onto fall, the days were still long but getting shorter. Her favorite time of year. At least it used to be. Before.

She stood, rising in a graceless lurch, leaning for a minute with her hand on the cross, making believe it was his shoulder. She bent down and kissed it, the painted wood a far cry from his downy, little boy cheek.

"It hasn't been downy for years, Mom."

She rolled her eyes. "I know, you're a grown man. Don't expect me to ever get used to it. See you tomorrow, kiddo."

"I'll be here."

She made it back to her car without turning around. She never turned around when she visited Trey—it would kill the illusion, chase away with logic the almost-certainty that he stood at her shoulder each time she visited and silence his voice forever.

She climbed into the Jeep Wrangler that Trey had been so excited about, back when she'd bought it, and pulled into traffic with what was probably excessive caution. It came with the job. Adjusting claims for a living, Chris had seen what a moment of inattention or haste could do to a human body.

She felt a stab of pain again thinking of Trey. How his body had ended up here, broken and bloodied, was a mystery. A single-car accident two years ago, a few months shy of his twenty-second birthday. No adverse road conditions, no driver impairment, no cell phone involvement. His Camaro—the car he'd begged for and worked since he was sixteen to help pay for—stranded, nose crumpled into the earth with the force of the impact. Trey, no seat belt, was launched through the shattered windshield, neck broken on impact with the tree his cross now stood under.

The way the cops at the scene, the doctors, even former friends, had latched onto that lack of seat belt as though that evened things out—as though it made it right that her son had died. There had to be something, some extenuating circumstance that could explain it. Something to separate her loss from their lives, so they wouldn't have to face the same thing she'd avoided facing all those years she'd had with him. *That it can be you. That one day, one night, you might get that call.*

She pushed it aside, refusing to let those images make a home in her head. Instead, she thought of Trey at his high school graduation, with the mohawk his father hated. His grin as he hugged Chris one-armed. There, much better. She kept her focus on the memory of that grin until she made it home.

She pulled into the drive for the little, one-and-a-half story, brick place she'd moved to when Trey started high school. It was in a better district, and she'd liked living somewhere they'd chosen together. The kitchen light was on, the way she always left it in the mornings, so she wouldn't come home to total darkness. There was no garage, just the drive, and the house was on a court, so she saw Dan sitting on his back deck in the near dark. He raised a hand, and his pit mix, Tootsie, sat up and thumped her tail.

"Hey, Dan. Hey, Toots."

"Chris. How are you?"

"I'm good," she said, because it was what she always said.

"It's a nice night," he called when she started to go inside. "Want to come have a beer?"

"Rain check," she said, without even thinking about it. "I'm beat."

"Hold you to it," he said, and she waved, trying not to feel bad about the note of disappointment in his voice. Dan was a nice guy, a lifelong bachelor who'd been living there since long before Chris moved in. He wasn't bad looking, either—thick dark hair, eyes a bright blue behind his glasses, a Tom Selleck mustache. He'd been trying to get her to go out with him for years, especially after Trey had moved out. She'd been over to his place a couple of times and always enjoyed herself, but it just seemed like so damn much trouble.

Or was it really that, she wondered as she let herself in through the kitchen door, set her purse on the counter, and her keys in the dish. How much trouble could it possibly be to drop her things off, check her makeup and her breath, and walk all of ten yards next door? It wasn't like Chris was a hermit—she leaned toward introverted, but that didn't mean she liked always being alone.

Part of it was the way Dan's presence silenced Trey's voice. Or rather, his voice in her head, the ongoing conversation she manufactured each night once she got home. Like being at the cross—pretending he was just out of sight, over her shoulder, in the kitchen, or thundering down the stairs from his bedroom. So many of their exchanges had taken place like that when he was alive—shouted across the house, spoken through open doors, disembodied voices that nevertheless connected multiple times a day. That made it easier, now, to ignore the looming dark truth that her son was dead. Gone, never to return.

No. Shove it away. Don't look at it, she thought as her chest tightened, her airway beginning to constrict. "I'm home," she called, as though it wasn't just for the benefit of the little white cat who came running from the living room.

The cat gave an inflected chirp as she jumped onto the kitchen table, and Chris picked her up. "Get off, Penny Lane. You're not allowed up there."

The cat was a stray Trey had brought home four years before. He found her, sopping wet and almost too small to survive, on the site of a construction gig he'd worked that summer. He was grown by then, a nineteen-year-old man, but he still looked to Chris to save the cat, to make things right, with a trust that took her breath away at the time.

5

She went to the pantry, opened the food container, and gave Penny a scoop. The cat purred while she ate, with a gratitude unusual in her species.

Chris went to the fridge, then closed it again when nothing appealed to her. She stood at the sink, looking out into the backyard, and wondered if Dan had food. He usually did. He was a good cook, and it was grilling season. Probably burgers or hot dogs, at the very least. Her stomach growled, and she opened the fridge door again. Nothing new and enticing having appeared, she made a decision.

Three minutes later, having popped two mints but skipped the makeup, Chris was tapping on the fence between her backyard and Dan's, a paper plate of dark chocolate brownies in hand. She didn't like cooking, but baking was another story. She loved the way the smell permeated the whole house, crept up the stairs and woke her sleeping son. How he'd come trailing down from his bedroom and sit in the kitchen with her, waiting for the day's treat to come out of the oven. She still baked every week, which was at least part of the reason for the way her jeans squeezed at her hips and thighs. She didn't much care about that; she'd just gone and bought new jeans when she noticed. She wasn't going to go through life uncomfortable, and the baking made her happy.

Dan looked up and smiled. "Change your mind?"

"Depends."

"On?"

"What's on offer."

His brows went up, a hopeful expression on his face until he noticed the plate in her hand. He smiled again. "No dinner again, huh?"

"None to speak of," she answered. *Shameless,* she heard in Trey's voice, just over her left shoulder, but still with that grin. She didn't realize she'd grinned back until Dan asked her what was funny.

"Nothing. Me, I guess. Shamelessly over here begging for food."

His smile widened, his teeth neat and white under his mustache, and he came to take the plate from her. Tootsie stood, stretched, and came to her side, knowing a soft touch when she saw one.

"C'mon up and have a seat—I'll fix you a plate."

He did better than that, and it was with a full stomach that she joined him on the wicker porch swing on the back deck, a beer in hand. Dan drank dark beer; she'd never seen him with anything else. But he always kept wheat beer in his fridge, which was the only kind Chris liked.

They sat in companionable silence for a while, Tootsie curled up beneath the swing, and Chris thought about going home. Already she was missing Trey, his voice, the way she didn't have to pretend not to be pretending. But it was nice here, too—the weather just cool enough to be comfortable, and Dan smelled good, something with sandalwood, maybe.

"D'you go today?" he asked, and she nodded.

"Most every day." That was something she liked about Dan—he knew about her daily ritual and never made her feel like it was weird, or something she needed to overcome. There were a couple of times she thought someone had been weeding over there, or cutting some of the overgrowth back, and she wondered if it was him. It seemed like something he'd do.

"And, how was he?"

"Same as always."

"Mm." He let the silence sit for a beat or two. "Glad you changed your mind—Toots and I haven't seen much of you the last little bit."

She scrubbed a hand across her face and sighed. "Yeah. We lost two adjusters recently, so I'm picking up the slack until we get replacements trained."

He listened, told her about his work when the opportunity presented itself, and Chris accepted another beer. One thing led to another, as it had from time to time over their long acquaintance, and he was leaning over kissing her, one hand grasping the chain of the porch swing just above hers. He tasted good, dark and malty, and he was always careful to wipe the foam from his mustache before he kissed her. She was tempted to stay, had almost accepted his unspoken invitation, when she saw a shadow move through her kitchen window.

Her breath caught; she waited. Dan was murmuring something in her ear, but she didn't hear it—there it was again, movement, over by the sink. There the shadow stayed, out of sight, but by now she knew someone was there.

She sat up, made her excuses, barely heard Dan's disappointed response. It would have been smart to tell him what was up, since what her heart was hoping for wasn't in the realm of possibility, but she couldn't do it; couldn't risk bringing him over. Her stomach roiling, breath coming shallow, she made her way across the yards and to her back door. When she glanced back, Dan was watching her, barely visible in the moonless dark. She stepped inside, breath held, and waited to see.

"Chris?"

She didn't register her name at first, just the voice that called to her from the kitchen, and it damn near stopped her heart. She took two trembling steps before reality fell on her like an anvil, and she recognized her ex-husband's aftershave.

For a moment it hurt so bad she couldn't breathe, couldn't answer him, and she wondered if this was it, if her heart would finally give out as she'd been expecting it to every day since Trey's death. But of course, it didn't, and she made herself take a breath and step into the kitchen, arms crossed over her chest.

"Beau. What're you doing here?"

Beau was leaning against the sink, his back to the window with a glass of wine in hand. He didn't like her kind of wine—white, sweet—but Beau would drink anything on offer, with the exception of bourbon. "Your door was open. Thought I'd see how you were."

Acting like he hadn't been watching her through the window, Chris thought, but didn't bring it up. "No, it wasn't," she said instead, getting a glass for herself and reaching across him for the bottle. He'd left it on the counter instead of putting it back in the fridge, which was irritating, but not as much as when they'd lived together.

He grinned behind his glass, one side of his mouth creeping higher than the other, a wolfish canine appearing over his lip. Beau was aging well, the eight-year age gap between them closing swiftly as he grayed gracefully. "Busted." He didn't look the least bit sorry.

"You're only supposed to use the key in case of emergency," she said, without hope of being listened to. She went to the table and sat down, and he settled in the chair across from her. Her lip twitched—it was Trey's seat, but she reminded herself it didn't matter.

"I know." He was giving her the overgrown schoolboy look that had never worked on her, even when she was young and in love.

"And is there an emergency?"

He frowned down at his glass and her heart sank. Fuck. Not this again.

"I came by because I was worried."

Chris sighed and sat back. "I'm fine, Beau."

"It's next week," he said, like he hadn't heard her.

"You think I don't know that?" she snapped. She felt light pressure on her left shoulder, and it reminded her to chill.

Beau was looking at her, his mouth turned down, hurt in his eyes. Trey had been his son, too, she told herself, and she took a deep breath before speaking again.

"I remember the anniversary, Beau. It sucks, but I'm okay."

He nodded, looked down at his glass again. "It's just that Nat saw your car again on the way home. It was getting dark, and she was worried. I was worried."

Chris bit her lip. *Tell Nat to call me when she's got a dead kid to visit.* She wouldn't say it. It wasn't fair to Beau, or his wife, who was actually a sweet girl. Chris knew she meant well. By the time Beau had met and married Natalie Temple, who was fifteen years his junior and seven years younger than Chris, their own marriage had been long over. They'd managed to skip over most of the drama that goes along with combining families, and Chris liked Natalie. Trey had too, though he'd been a moody teen at the time, and Chris liked to think that had something to do with the good job she and Beau had done co-parenting since their split when Trey was two. Trey had been apprehensive when Natalie got pregnant, but they'd had a long talk about how he'd have the best of both worlds—an only child at Chris's, and siblings at Beau's. He'd ended up loving his two young half-sisters, in large part because Natalie had been savvy and thoughtful in the way she included Trey, and Chris had enjoyed getting photo updates on the girls from her smitten son.

She sometimes wondered if Lana and Emily were why Beau had seemed to have an easier time coming to terms with Trey's death. It was another one of those things she'd never say out loud, but she thought even Beau would have agreed. He'd told her, during one of those hazy, hellish sob sessions in the early days after the accident, that they should have had more kids after Trey, that it would have made things easier for her. She knew he hadn't meant it to sound the way it had, as though Trey could be replaced, his absence mitigated, and she supposed that for him it was true. Not that he hadn't loved his son, but after the visitation and the funeral, that surreal graveside service when they'd put their boy in the ground, he'd gone home to his wife and held his living, breathing daughters. Chris knew that was what was on his mind, so she forgave him, but she had never wanted anything but Trey, and losing him hadn't changed that.

"Please tell Natalie thank you, but I'm coping." Nat would like that word. She was a counselor, though she usually refrained from wielding it against her family. "It's not unusual to spend time at a loved one's grave, especially a child's."

She nearly flinched at the kick of betrayal stirred up by her own words, as though Trey would be wounded at the idea of his death. *He* is *dead,* she told herself, even as she turned her face from the words and tucked them elsewhere out of sight.

Beau still wasn't looking at her—he'd always had a hard time talking about feelings, but it was kind of him to make the effort. "It's not even his grave, Chris. Trey's not buried there, it's just where he...and it can't be healthy, spending so much time where...where *that* happened."

Chris raised a shoulder. "It's where I feel close to him," she said. "I don't like cemeteries, you know that."

He nodded, finally met her eyes. "You still get those dreams?" he asked, his expression softened. He was back on safer ground now, their shared history, the small things he still knew about her from the time before everything hurt so much.

She grimaced. "Not as much as I used to," she lied. "It's still unpleasant."

Chris had dreamed for years now of suffocation, of sliding beneath a soft surface of dirt and dying as the air was pressed from her lungs. Night terrors ran in her family, and when she and Beau were still together, he'd had to wake her as she thrashed and screamed. She wasn't sure where the dreams had come from— to her knowledge, she'd never had personal experience with suffocation, and she wasn't claustrophobic. It had been with her as long as she could remember, and after the first time she'd attended a graveside interment, the dreams had changed to accommodate this new wrinkle. Now, it was always in a cemetery at night. Chris would be at a grave head, unable to read the inscription. She would move closer, bending down to get a look, and the ground would open up, swallow her whole, filling her mouth with dirt. She'd barely made it through Trey's service, sweating and hyperventilating the whole time, but no one had thought her behavior out of line. It was, after all, her own son's funeral.

Beau nodded and drained half his glass. "Good. I was afraid it might get worse, you know, after..."

She sighed. "Yeah, I know. Tell Nat I appreciate it, and that I said hi." She stood, and after a minute he did, too. She walked him to the door, not touching, but sensing his deflation, his sadness. She knew he'd be hurting too, this close to the anniversary of their son's death, but she didn't have it in her to talk him through it. He had Natalie for that.

He gave her a lingering hug and stopped on the top step. "You should come over. We're going to cook out—steaks and hot dogs. The girls would love to see you, and you don't need to be on your own."

Chris gave him a tight smile, arms wrapped round her middle. "Maybe. I might be working late."

He nodded and walked to his car, giving her a wave as he pulled out of her drive. Chris glanced over at Dan's and thought she might have seen him watching out his own kitchen window. She went inside and sat in the darkened living room, waiting for the pain to hit her. Instead, a weight settled at the other end of the couch and she flipped on the television.

"Up for a horror movie?" she asked.

A snort, from a place just out of sight. "When am I not, Mom?"

CHAPTER TWO

When Chris woke, it was with the feeling of having just missed something. A voice seemed to still hang in the dark of her bedroom, and she sat up, waiting for it to come again. The house was silent.

She got up to pee without turning on the light, but hesitated before returning to bed. She was tired, but she felt like she'd been woken for a reason. She went to the closest of the two big windows that faced the street and leaned against the glass, cooled in the way the early morning air does as summer lets go. She stared out with the expectation of being disappointed, as she always was.

Except she wasn't.

Because he was standing there. In the pool of castoff light from the streetlamp that stood at the front-most edge of her yard. His hands dug into the pockets of his sagging jeans, hair sliding over his eye. He was real, and solid, and he was smiling up at her. And as she stared at him, breath frozen in her lungs, refusing to blink, he raised a hand and waved, with that goofy little finger wiggle he'd perfected when he'd stopped wanting her to kiss him in front of his school, but still wanted to communicate to her that he loved her.

If the window had been open, she'd have jumped out of it in her haste to get to him. She couldn't take her eyes off him, so going out the front door wasn't an option, but as she fumbled with the latch, her gaze dropped for a millisecond. When she looked up again, he wasn't gone, as she'd been sure he would be, but instead was shaking his head and laughing. She couldn't hear it, but she could see it, in the tremor of his shoulders and the duck of his head. He blew her a kiss, turned and walked away into shadow. She watched until her eyes burned, but he never reappeared.

CHAPTER THREE

C hris spent the rest of the night at the window huddled in a blanket on the divan she'd pulled from its place by the closet. Trey never showed back up, either outside or in her head—he hadn't popped up to chide her or to talk her back to a sense of reality. It bothered her, a little, but it also increased the importance of the sighting. It had to mean something that her pretend interaction with her son had gone quiet—it had really, truly been him out there. No doubt in her mind, and no mistaking it for someone else, someone who just looked like her boy. Who else would be waiting outside her house in the middle of the night, laughing and waving his special wave? The question wasn't, how is this possible, or what does this mean? No, the question was, how did she get him to come back?

Early morning found her at the kitchen table, still wrapped in the soft red Sherpa blanket Trey had gotten her for Christmas four years ago. She was on her laptop, a cup of cinnamon coffee in front of her, researching ghost sightings. It wasn't new material for her. Chris had always loved ghost stories, and she was a sucker for books and movies about the supernatural. Beau, who'd always despised the horror genre, used to ask her how she could stand to suffer through so many crappy movies. He hadn't believed her when she'd told him that the shittiest horror movie was light-years ahead of a football game, any day of the week. It had been something else Trey had gotten from her—a love of the macabre. They used to have movie marathons he wouldn't tell his father about. All the classics, plus new ones he'd recommended.

Then when Trey was gone, Chris had launched into research mode. She believed in ghosts—she always had, and she fixated on the idea that Trey could come back to her, if she just wanted it enough. She looked for him everywhere, listened in the stillness of the night. She did tarot card readings, went to psychics, and bought an Ouija board. When none of that netted any results, she started watching ghost hunter shows and true hauntings. Taking comfort in the stories of others who'd been blessed—or cursed—with visits from the beyond.

By the time Trey had been gone for six months, Chris had stopped believing she'd see him. She still watched the shows, but preferred the ones that focused on helping the people who were haunted. *Paranormal Warriors* was one of her favorites. She lost herself in watching the adventures of two brothers, the youngest, Alex, purporting to be a psychic, his elder brother Greg acting as his protector, and reminding her so much of Trey. Netflix had a backlog of episodes and even if she didn't always buy the supernatural flavor of the week, the boys seemed like they truly cared about the people who asked for their help. She thought it might have been something Trey would have enjoyed. Or maybe he'd have poked fun at it—she'd have given anything to watch it with him.

She wasn't sure when it had changed. Somewhere in there, it went from her wishing and imagining, to feeling real. Their conversations grew longer, more frequent, and by the time of the first anniversary of his death, she could go weeks without having to remember he was gone. So, her research and obsession had fallen off, and she'd seen that as a positive development.

Today though, she was back on it. What had brought him back, now? Was it the approaching anniversary? Could she expect him to come again? Would this become a yearly thing? Her heart raced at the idea of it. A yearly visit from Trey—she would never ask for anything more if she could have that.

By the time she had to leave for work, she'd found nothing useful. Everything having to do with ghosts was purely anecdotal, and folks believed in all kinds of theories about why they might return. She was distracted all day, her mind with Trey out under the streetlight. She hardly made it through the final hours at the office, and when Dan called her name as she climbed out of the Jeep, she barely stopped to wave. She could have gone over, she knew—she'd need a distraction to get her through to bedtime, but she was afraid to be away from the house. Instead, she settled in, watched *The Thing*, *The Exorcist*, and *Poltergeist*, then dragged herself up to bed, setting her alarm for the same time Trey appeared the previous night. Even though part of her was convinced he'd find a way to wake her again, she didn't want to take any chances.

But when the time came, when the alarm went off and she stumbled to the front window, there was nothing. She watched for the rest of the night, hope dying an inch at a time but hanging on until the sun came up, and the spot under the streetlight stayed empty. That morning she came down the stairs, heavy with grief, disconcerted to realize how hard this had hit her. It was all she could do to make the coffee, opting for instant since she was too tired to use the coffee pot. She seriously considered calling into work, but the knowledge of how far behind she was on cases pushed her out the door. That, and the reality that if she didn't go to work, she'd just lie around the house all day feeling sad. She was afraid to do that for a number of reasons, primary among them being the realization that her son's voice hadn't returned. She wanted to believe it was a result of her preoccupation, but Chris was afraid.

That night, she stopped at the roadside cross again. It was six nights until the anniversary, and her heart was thumping as she descended into the hollow. The leaves had started to turn, and a swell of them had gathered against the cross's base. Chris pushed them aside and waited, but as the sun went down, Trey stayed silent.

She tried holding up her end of the conversation—speaking to him as she always had, a running commentary peppered with sarcasm—but her mind was silent when it came his time to speak. She grew frustrated, then panicked. She didn't understand how this could happen—it had always been a daydream anyway, her own imagination supplying Trey's answers, formulated from a lifetime of listening to her son, pulling his words in and holding them close. How could her own mind close her out of the fantasy she needed to survive? Because that's what it was: survival. If Chris had to face the knowledge head on that her son was dead, she would drop to her knees and give up.

Angry tears marring her face, she climbed up to her car in full darkness. No doubt she'd hear from Beau again, more concern from Natalie that she was wallowing, but what the hell else was she supposed to do? There was no moving on, she knew that now. There was only the hope that she'd see Trey again, a hope that had been raised and trashed in the last thirty-six hours.

That night she turned her phone off, locked her doors, and turned off the lights. Exhausted, but not tired enough to escape the torturous loop of pain that awaited her inactive brain, she curled up on the couch in her blanket and binged old episodes of *Paranormal Warriors*. They soothed her and pushed the pain to a place just out of sight, easing the ache in her chest enough to let her breathe again.

She must have dozed off, waking in the early hours to a paused screen with Netflix's question about whether she was still there. She rubbed her eyes, reached for the remote, and confirmed her existence. The episode resumed and she tried to figure out which one it was. It seemed to be one about demon infestations, which she didn't care for as much, but she couldn't be bothered to search for something else.

She was nearly asleep again when the brothers' raised voices roused her. A phrase caught her attention; she sat up, heart pounding. Had she heard right?

"A crossroads demon?" Greg asked, one hand on his brother's chest, pushing him back, away from danger.

Chris sat back. She hadn't heard right—she'd thought they'd said something about a roadside cross, which called to mind her son's. That wasn't it, though. She remembered the episode—the brothers had been called in to help an old man who'd supposedly made a deal decades before. It was one of the silliest shows they'd done, and the least believable.

Still, the idea of the crossroads demon was an interesting one. She was familiar with the old story about blues legend Robert Johnson, the one that claimed he'd summoned a demon at the crossroads, ostensibly exchanging his soul for his musical talents. Stemming from a song he'd written, the story had become part of his mythology, one Chris had always thought had more to do with effective marketing than an actual Faustian bargain.

She swiped at her eyes, wishing she believed in such things. Ghosts, certainly, Chris had no problem with that. God, as well. She'd been a believer from the time she was a small child, and even when things were at their worst, it didn't take her away from Him. She'd never believed that faith could save her family or protect her from the agony of loss she now suffered. Things didn't work that way, though she had sympathy for parents who turned their back when their children were taken. But demons were just make believe, a tool to frighten the religious masses into subservience. Anyway, even if she did believe in demons, she'd always thought it was a stupid trope. Who in their right mind would trade their immortal soul for any kind of earthly pleasure? It didn't make sense.

Except, of course, that these days, she could easily name something for which she'd trade her soul.

She wasn't sure when the idea took hold, or even what she meant to do with it, but at some point that night she went to retrieve a notepad and pen, jotting down a few things, and when the credits rolled, she went back and played the episode again. When it had finished for a second time, she halted the autoplay feature and sat chewing a thumbnail in the dark.

It was stupid, she told herself. A joke. An almost certainly fictitious account with nothing to back it up, and she didn't even believe in demons. But she thought back to the day before the night she'd seen Trey. She'd been to the cross, stayed a while, done her usual thing. She'd cut herself, she remembered, and it was her blood that had sparked the internal conversation with Trey.

She stared into the dark, remembering the way her blood had seeped into the dried ground. Thought of burying something to summon a demon and make a trade.

Chris didn't believe that was what had happened—there'd been no trade, no demon, and nothing evil or wrong about the way her son had manifested that night. He'd seemed happy, normal, his old self. But there was no escaping that the difference had been her blood, shed in the ground where her son had died.

She used to bring things out there in the early days, like she'd seen others do. Usually when she'd seen roadside crosses in the past, there were wreaths of flowers, words of remembrance.

She'd brought flowers a couple of times, but they'd wilted quickly, and somehow had added to the depression of the place. Once, she'd used an idea she'd seen in one of the Facebook support groups she was a member of and brought one of Trey's t-shirts out there. She'd placed it on the cross, and at first, she'd kind of liked it. It was one of his favorite shirts, from a Clutch show Beau had taken him to when he was a teenager. Seeing the shirt filled out by the arms of the cross, the way it billowed as the breeze rushed across it, could almost make her believe he was wearing it again. But when she'd gotten in her car and looked back, the image jolted her. It looked like a headless torso was half-buried in the ground, and she scrambled out to take the shirt back. That was the last time she'd tried decoration of any kind.

But this wasn't about decoration; it was about an offering. What was Johnson purported to have buried to summon the demon in the first place? She pulled her phone out and searched, but it soon became clear that it wasn't part of the legend, that the burying thing was part of a larger, more nebulous canon. The *Paranormal Warriors* Wiki page informed her that you needed to bury a box containing a picture of the mortal wanting to make the deal, some graveyard dirt, and the bone of a black cat.

She sat back. Well, that was just silly. Chris sure as hell wasn't going to commit cat murder based on anything from Wiki, and in any case, she didn't want to make a deal with a demon. She heard the jingle of a tiny bell and looked up to find Penny Lane's glowing eyes on hers in the darkness. She reached out to scratch the cat's ears. "Anyway, it said a black cat, so you're safe," Chris told her.

No animal cruelty, no. But if it were a matter of an offering, she could handle that. So, what should she bury?

Feeling stupid and hopeful in equal measures, she climbed the stairs to her bedroom and rummaged through her jewelry box. She'd never been one for expensive pieces, and the most valuable item she owned was likely her engagement ring. It was a large, flawed diamond in a yellow gold setting that she'd never much cared for but hadn't had the heart to tell Beau. She fished it out from the bottom of the box and looked it over. It wasn't much, but it was what she had, and it didn't matter to her if she never saw it again.

As exhausted as she was after several nights of broken sleep, Chris still had trouble drifting off that night, thinking about getting out to the cross the next day. It was a Saturday, and she'd brought some files home, but she didn't have a set schedule so she could go out as early as she liked. She awoke, groggy, just after seven, and headed out with a travel mug of instant coffee and the ring in a plastic baggie in her jeans pocket.

When she'd buried the ring at the base of Trey's cross, she sat back and drank her coffee in the shade. It was early enough to be quiet, with only the occasional car zipping past. She knew what she was doing would fall into the category of delusion, but she couldn't help herself. It was five days until the anniversary, and she felt like that meant something; she only had so long to solve the puzzle or her window would close. She stayed until the growling of her belly threatened to make her sick, then she brushed herself off and went to breakfast at Cracker Barrel, where she ordered the blackberry pancakes because it was what Trey had always gotten.

That night she set her alarm for the same time he'd visited before, feeling like a kid on Christmas morning when it went off and she hurried to the window. But again, she was disappointed, because there was no one under the streetlight. Not when she woke, and not in any of the hours she sat up waiting.

CHAPTER FOUR

Over the next three days, Chris went back to the cross with new offerings each time. Deciding that the value of the item might be relative, she started burying things that had belonged to her son. It was hard, at first. She hadn't wanted to let go of anything that had belonged to him, not so much as a pair of his socks, but she wondered if that was what was needed—something that represented a true sacrifice. Then, too, since she didn't believe in the idea of a demon anyway, cross-roads or otherwise, she thought she might as well mix her mythology up further and consider her offerings as gifts for Trey in the afterlife. She knew the idea would have made his eyes roll nearly out of his head, and in part maybe she'd done it to see if she could kick-start his voice back into her head, but it hadn't worked.

She'd started with that Clutch t-shirt, and her stomach had done flips all the way to the cross. She told herself it wasn't for-ever, and that if it didn't work, which of course it wouldn't, she could just dig the shirt back up and take it home.

Except that when she searched for the diamond ring, it was gone. She didn't believe it at first, assuming it must have somehow been pushed further into the ground, but when she'd dug down two feet, and widened the area well beyond where it could have traveled, she had to admit defeat.

She sat back on her heels, hands and knees covered in dirt. Where the fuck had it gone? It was possible someone had stolen it, but it seemed unlikely. The ground had been packed flat when she'd arrived, same as she'd left it the day before. Someone could have been careful to pat the dirt back to cover the theft, but who the hell would think of coming out to this isolated place and digging for buried treasure in the first place?

It didn't matter. However it had happened, the damned thing was gone. It hurt a little—she didn't hold onto much nostalgia for her marriage. It had been good until it wasn't, and it was her choice to split up. She'd done it before she got a chance to hate him, but she never phrased it that way to Beau. There had been some pain, at the beginning, but never a question of whether she'd been right to do it. And anyway, it was all years ago now, so she didn't know why it bothered her at all. Maybe it was just about losing another part of her history.

What bothered her more, as the sun climbed higher overhead, was the chance of losing Trey's things. She looked at the shirt she'd brought with her, softened from so many washings, and thought of never seeing it, never touching it again. If it brought Trey to her, it would be worth it. But what if it didn't? What if she buried this precious thing, and he didn't show up, and she came back here tomorrow, and it was gone? Could she live with that?

Tears filled her eyes at the thought, and as her mind rolled back, she thought of how hard it had been to get pregnant in the first place. The years it had taken, the increasingly invasive tests and procedures. Some of them painful, all of them expensive, both financially and emotionally. And never with a guarantee of success. Chris knew, somewhere in the middle of that hellish road, that once she set her foot upon it, she might be doomed to walk it forever. She might never get her baby, and though that hurt had passed when she'd finally gotten pregnant, she still remembered it. She would always remember, and be grateful that she'd kept going, guarantee or not.

Maybe this was the same principle. Whether or not her sacrifice would bring her what she wanted, she would carry it out anyway. She took a breath, knowing how far down the spiral of magical thinking she'd gone, but unable to find a reason to pull out of it. So, she folded her son's favorite shirt, pressed a final kiss to the fabric, and began to bury it in the hole she'd dug. She tried not to feel like she was burying him again, but somehow, she did.

CHAPTER FIVE

Trey didn't come that night. Or the night after that, or the night after that. Chris had faithfully attended the cross each morning, getting up early enough to go before work once Monday rolled around, but he never showed himself, and none of the things she buried were ever there when she dug. She'd cried bitter tears that first morning when she couldn't find his shirt. Her world, her wants, had winnowed down to this tiny thing, this shadow of the love that had once been hers. She was desperate to get it back, to feel it again in her hands, but it wasn't there.

In some ways, that made burying his class ring easier. Not because it wouldn't hurt to lose, but Chris was unable to convince herself that someone had stolen, on two separate occasions, a ring and a t-shirt from the ground beneath Trey's cross. Her logic being what it was at the moment, it had to mean she was communicating with *something*, that someone had heard her calls and was accepting her offerings. She thought again of the crossroads demon, but again dismissed it as fancy. Chris didn't believe in demons. They were silly.

Again, the ground accepted the class ring without giving her anything back. Again, she returned, this time with what she felt sure must summon Trey if anything could. She sat in the middle of the turned earth and cradled the little box close to her chest, the one that held the locks from his first haircut, and several of his baby teeth. She cried to think of losing them, these last traces of her boy. Once they were gone, she'd never be able to touch a part of him that had once been alive, not ever. It hurt like hell to let go, but she did it, praying and begging the whole time.

Nothing.

Chris was alone that night, as she had been every night since her son's death, and she railed against the unfairness of it, and her own stupidity. She wandered the darkened house in a rage, sobbing so hard she couldn't breathe. In that haze, she listened for Trey's voice, but was met with silence that seemed eternal. She stared down the barrel of years of that silence and wished for the courage to end her own life.

The next morning, before the sun made its appearance, Chris was back at the cross. She hadn't slept, and she felt light-headed but calm. Her face was swollen from crying, but no tears fell now. She looked at the undisturbed ground, hands in her lap, but today she didn't even bother digging. She knew it would be gone, the precious box, but she didn't care anymore. She knew now what she had to do.

Chris hugged the cross, and kissed it, making believe it was Trey one last time. Breath hitching, she took the kitchen knife, one of the nice ones Beau had left her when he moved out, sharpened and ready. She began to draw the blade down her arm, not across, as she knew from countless television shows and books, and had seen firsthand at a few fatalities. She started strong, the blade biting deep into the flesh just below her elbow, but it hurt more than she expected. She gasped and stopped, mesmerized by the sheet of crimson that rolled down her arm.

A honk sounded somewhere far above her, then a car door slammed, and someone called her name.

"Chris?"

She dropped the knife and nudged it behind her even as she cursed Natalie's timing. She rolled the sleeve of her sweatshirt down, stuffing a wad of tissues from her pocket up it at the same time. There was no way it would staunch the flow for long, but maybe it would be enough to get rid of the other woman.

"Chris?" Nat called again, descending the embankment in little side steps. She managed it in heels, and Chris admired her balance.

"Hey, Nat," she said, not bothering to keep the exhaustion from her voice. Just another few minutes, and she could rest.

Nat stopped a few feet away, her round face pinched with worry. "Chris, honey, what're you doing down here so early? It's barely even light out."

Chris wiped her eyes with her uninjured hand. "Talking to him," she said. "It's what I come here to do."

Natalie hesitated, then knelt next to her in the dirt, with no concern for her slacks or shoes. It was one of the things that had always made it hard to hate her, even if Chris had been so inclined. She was a better dresser, but when the shit hit the fan, she never gave her appearance a second thought.

They sat in silence for a minute or so. Chris knew Nat was being respectful, and at any other time she'd have been appreciative, maybe even enjoyed the company. But today she just wanted her to fuck off so she could finish what she came here to do.

"Is it helping?" asked Nat in a low voice.

Chris bit her lip. She didn't have the energy to break down. "No."

Nat's hand went to her shoulder, squeezed. "I'm fucking sorry, Chris. I know that doesn't mean a thing right now. But I am. Trey was a beautiful boy."

Chris sighed. "He was."

"Chris? What the hell is wrong with your arm?"

She moved it out of sight. "Nothing, not a big deal. I slipped with a kitchen knife last night, must have opened back up."

Natalie grabbed her hand. "Ya think? Holy shit, girl, your sleeve is soaked. You've bled a bucket into the ground here. Let me see it."

Chris yanked her arm away. "No, I told you, it's fine."

Natalie held her gaze. "Come on. We need to get that bandaged again. You might need stitches."

Chris could have screamed at the unfairness of it, but when she would have argued, she thought she felt it again, that light pressure on her left shoulder.

Trey, she thought, flooded with relief. Trey was still there, and he wanted her to go with Natalie. As she got to her feet, using the cross for leverage, she realized it made sense. However much she might want to give up, to end things so she could be with her boy, it would never be what Trey would want. He'd sent Natalie to her, just in time. She didn't know how to feel about losing her opportunity, but she had always, at every turn, done what was best for her son. No matter how hard, how much it cost her personally, she'd never backed down. She wouldn't start now.

She let Natalie help her up the embankment and stopped at the top. She looked back when she heard the leaves rustling behind her. She smiled. Anyone else would have called it a breeze, but she knew better. She knew her own boy's voice.

CHAPTER SIX

She wasn't surprised that night when she was woken from a dead and dreamless sleep in the small hours of the morning. It was the same as before, the same sense of words spoken, still ringing in the atmosphere of the room. She went to the window, and there he was.

She could have wept. She would have wept; except she didn't want to greet her boy with a tragic face. And in any case, as soon as she saw him—standing closer this time, surely?—all was well with her again. Her heart returned to the precarious peace she'd crafted over the last two years, and she was able to smile and return his wave. She raised her eyebrows, pointed to the street, but he shook his head and smiled, so she stayed where she was, content to look at him.

He cocked his head, lifted his arm, and patted it in the same place she'd cut herself. His forehead wrinkled and his mouth turned down.

She shook her head and gave him a thumbs up. She was fine, and he must have gotten the message, as his smile returned. He stayed another few minutes and then he gave that wave again, blew her a kiss, and once more disappeared into the shadows. She settled into the divan where she'd left it by the window, and fell asleep in an instant, the worst of her worries lifted by his gift.

CHAPTER SEVEN

The next day was the anniversary. Two years since she got the call that would forever change her life. Terrified but focused, because at that point there'd still been hope— they hadn't found him yet. She had a vague memory of that Chris, the one who'd asked the right questions of the dispatcher, who'd thrown on clothes, and driven in a strange, cold clarity to look for her boy. The Chris who'd died forever when they'd found him in the tree, taking him down just as she arrived. Two years since the last morning all had felt right in her world. But that wasn't how she thought of it when she woke and knew what day it was. Instead, that morning felt like a rebirth, as though all the mornings in between had been a nightmare from which she'd finally woken.

She knew now it had nothing to do with the date. Trey hadn't returned because of an arbitrary calendar flip, but because of a blood sacrifice. Hers. She'd known that since she'd heard his whisper through the trees, looked down from above and saw the dark patch of soaked earth. None of the other sacrifices had been right because it had to be blood. Her blood, and she was happy to give it.

Her buoyancy carried her through the workday, and the inevitable call from Beau. It even prompted her to accept his renewed invitation to come over that evening. He sounded surprised but pleased, and told her Nat would be happy.

I imagine she will, thought Chris, with a stab of guilt. She'd given the other woman no explanation for her behavior or her injury, and she knew Nat would be worried. Well, Chris coming to dinner would mitigate that, and anyway, tonight she felt like celebrating Trey's life with other people who had loved him.

She had a better time than she'd expected. It was impossible not to be flattered when Lana and Emily both shrieked her name and came running when they saw her. She played with the girls, ate Beau's cooking, had two beers with Natalie, and went home on a contented cushion of good feeling. She'd cut out early from work and made her stop at the cross beforehand, left her offering, and had time to bind her bleeding ankle before dinner.

Her happiness even upheld her through a call from her mother, once she'd arrived home. She let it go to voicemail to give herself time to feed and love on Penny Lane and pour a glass of wine for herself. She hesitated over it—it was better if she didn't mix alcohol, but she was feeling so good, so *right*, she decided to take a chance. Two minutes in, she was glad to have it, though in truth the call wasn't as bad as it could have been. Not because Lenora cut her any slack—it took no time at all for her to make the anniversary, and the conversation, all about her. Chris's mother was good at that, but she was used to it, and even the forced tragic tone in which Lenora answered the phone didn't get under her skin the way it usually did.

It was Trey that made all that annoyance fade into the background, allowed her to converse and dodge the inevitable barbs Lenora fired as they spoke. It had always been her son who helped her to do it. Chris had grown up the only child of a narcissist and an alcoholic, and when her father's drinking tipped him into an early grave, she and her mother had become even more enmeshed. It had taken years for her to claw her way out from under the woman's heavy and toxic shadow. Beau had helped some, given her a sounding board and the validation she was never going to get from Lenora. But when Trey had come, the struggles and small victories had become easier. Chris's vision became crystal clear—her son was the most important person in her life, full stop, and she would always do what was right for him. It was easier to stand up in his defense than in her own, and she did it, over and over, until her mother got the point. The other benefit was that she was finally able to see, with heartbreaking clarity, that she'd never done anything to earn the disgust, disappointment, and sometimes outright hatred her mother showed her. Having her own child meant she knew there was nothing she *could* have done to earn it, and though it hurt, she'd let go of the idea that she and her mother would ever have a real relationship.

Since Trey's death, Chris's previous arms-length patience for Lenora had shattered, and she rarely spoke to her without ending up yelling or hanging up. But tonight, she was pleasant, and whatever Lenora may have felt, Chris hung up with her peace unimpaired.

Riding a pleasant buzz, she checked the time. Nine-thirty; a good chance Dan would still be up. She peeked from her kitchen window and saw him out on the porch. He saw her too and raised a hand, but he looked surprised when she opened the gates between their yards ten minutes later with a fresh wine bottle in hand. He stood and disappeared into the house when she climbed the porch and knelt to greet Tootsie, coming back outside with two glasses ten seconds later.

"What's the occasion?" he asked as she poured. He slapped

his forehead a second later. "Fuck. Oh goddamnit, Chris, I'm sorry. I know what the occasion is, I didn't forget, I just—"

She handed him a glass and took his free hand. "Dan. Chill with the self-flagellation. I appreciate that you remembered, but I'm not here about that."

When she settled on the porch swing, he sat next to her. "I always remember, Chris."

"I know." She could barely see his face, the porch was so dark, but she hadn't asked him to turn on a light. It was nice like this. Quiet, but the comfortable kind.

Dan cleared his throat. "We haven't seen much of you, the last week or so. Work still crazy?"

"It is, but I'm not here about that, either."

He cocked his head and leaned back. "Uh, okay, I feel like I'm making some missteps tonight, so why don't you tell me what you *do* want to talk about?"

She put her glass down, leaned over to kiss him. "What if I'm not here to talk at all?"

He damn near threw his own glass down, pulling her to him. "That's fine and dandy with me—we don't have to say another thing."

Later, when they managed to pull apart long enough for her to follow him to his bedroom, she stopped him in the door. "One caveat."

"Caveat?" He put his hand on his chest. "Oh, thank Christ. I thought you were about to call it off."

She smiled and stepped closer, pulling her shirt over her head, and tossing it to the floor. "Hell, no. I was just going to say, I can't spend the night."

The hazy look of worship he wore as his gaze traveled her body made her warm in all the right places. "Woman, I will take whatever you're willing to give, and I'll still bring you breakfast in the morning."

CHAPTER EIGHT

For the next six weeks, Chris's world was bliss. Each day, she'd go to work, stop by the cross to make her offering, spend her evening with Dan and Tootsie, then be up in the small hours for her nightly visit with Trey. It was a hectic schedule, with work getting more demanding all the time, and little of her hours with Dan spent sleeping, but she was running off that new love high. Not just Dan, although he was some of it, surely. He cooked for her, watched movies she enjoyed even though she knew he wasn't a horror fan, and purchased things for his house to make her more comfortable. And the sex was off the hook phenomenal. Chris knew how much of that had to do with how gorgeous and sexy he made her feel when she slipped her clothes off in the lamplight of his room. She'd never felt that sexy with Beau, and sure as shit not when she was alone and caught a glimpse of herself in the mirror.

So, some of it was Dan, but the largest part of her high was the same one she'd experienced when she brought Trey home from the hospital. Chris had never been able to nap, or sleep at all once the sun was up, so with the baby's reflux and erratic schedule, she'd spent the first weeks of his life running on an hour or two a day. But it was that love, the same love that gets you up and out the door to school as a teenager after spending all night on the phone with some boy. The love that gets you in the shower and to work after an all-night session with a new boy-friend. It was that high times a hundred, so even though it had damn near killed her back then, she'd done it.

And now it was so much more. Chris had always valued her son. It had taken all that time to get pregnant, and she'd had the advantage of being in a stable marriage, financially secure, and with only one child. She knew she'd been free of many of the stressors that can bog down a new mother, can strip her of her identity. She was damn lucky, and she knew it. She'd never taken Trey for granted, but to be given this unexpected gift, to get him back when he'd been gone, even if only for a few minutes a night, was the greatest high of all. She was tired, and dragging a little, but it was worth it. Every single second was worth it. She could have kept on like that forever, but it wasn't up to her. She should have known it was too good to last.

She started to notice Trey was coming later, and not staying as long. He'd been appearing at the same time every night, like clockwork, but then he was a minute late. Then two, then five. Those times made her panic, her breath coming quick as she searched the darkness for him. Each time he'd appeared, and her fear had evaporated, but then he would leave again, well before she was ready. Well, she was never ready, but when she brought her phone with her once and timed it, she knew she was right.

It wasn't just the time shortening, either. Trey was her boy, and even through the dark and distance that separated them, she could tell something was wrong. He looked paler, thinner; less substantial. And his demeanor was...she didn't want to say sullen, because that wasn't it, not quite. But he wasn't happy, and their interactions became touchier. Sometimes he spent the whole visit just staring up at her window, not smiling, not trying to make her laugh.

Dan had noticed as well. Not Trey himself—no one but Chris knew about those visits, though Dan had commented on her propensity for self-injury.

"Darlin', you cut yourself more than anyone I know. You training with throwing stars over there, or what?"

She'd laughed it off, blaming paper cuts, and kitchen knives, and shaving her legs, and every other damn thing, but she could tell he wasn't convinced. It was getting tiresome, a little, having to slice herself open each day, to spill enough blood to satisfy the thirsty ground. She knew it was worth it, though, so she gritted her teeth and kept going, doing what she could to mitigate the scars. Dan hadn't brought it up again, though he'd bought her slip proof knives and a safety razor. She'd just about cried when she opened the box—it was the most thoughtful gift anyone had ever given her, but Dan did that kind of thing all the time. He noticed what was bothering her, or causing a problem in her life, and he went about fixing it without saying a word. For that, and for the space he gave her without complaint, Chris knew she was falling in love with him.

As much as she trusted him though, she hadn't told him about Trey. She hadn't told anyone, not even Beau, although that made her feel guilty sometimes, wondering if he should be joining in these visits. But Dan had noticed the dip in her mood, the way she went quiet now, the worry around her eyes. He'd asked her what was wrong, but he hadn't seemed offended when she declined to take him into her confidence. She wasn't going to lie and say she was fine—she'd had a belly full of that shit when she was married, thank you very much. But it was her problem to solve, only she didn't have the slightest idea how. She didn't mind if Trey was moody sometimes, or if he wasn't able to stay as long, but she was afraid of what it meant for the long term. Was their time running out; their window closing? The idea brought that same grief and panic of the early days, but she didn't know what to do about it if that was the case.

When the problem persisted, to the point of Trey appearing for only two or three minutes the previous night, then sweeping into the darkness with his shoulders hunched, the strain was wearing her down. She was exhausted, unable to catch any more sleep after he had gone, and Dan noticed the dark circles under her eyes.

He cleared his throat. "You know," he said, casting a glance at her. "I usually find if I'm worried about somebody, it's best I just ask 'em directly what's wrong."

She stared at him blindly for a moment, then took a breath. "You're right. That's just what I'll do."

God knew who Dan might have had in mind, but Chris wrapped herself in her winter coat that night and waited for Trey by the streetlight.

She was nervous, checking the time every thirty seconds or so. She'd never done this before, and she didn't know how it might affect the visitation. She would have loved to have seen him up close long before this, maybe even touch him, but it had seemed an unspoken rule of the game that she stayed inside and viewed him from above. Maybe he wouldn't come with her waiting here. Maybe he'd never come again, the spell broken by her lack of faith, and she'd be grieving her ineptitude the rest of her days. But inertia had never been Chris's besetting sin—Beau had that one covered.

She didn't hear him coming, he was just there. She blinked, because she hadn't even seen him appear, or materialize or anything. He was there and speaking in the same breath.

"What're you doing down here, Mom?" he asked, looming over her, features pinched in a way that indicated pain, or annoyance.

Chris stopped, mouth open, looking up at him. She searched his face and was reassured—it was him, her Trey. It was only that, for a second there, it hadn't sounded like him.

His brows descended further. "What's wrong? Don't you know your own son?" he asked, reading her mind.

She shook it off, reached a hand out to touch his shoulder. He didn't stop her, and she gripped it, feeling the bone beneath. "Of course, I do."

"Then what're you doing here?"

"Waiting for you. Is it not okay? Am I not supposed to get this close?"

He shrugged and her hand slipped from his arm. "I don't know. I don't make the rules."

She frowned. "Then who does?"

He dug his hands in his pockets and looked up into the clear, dark sky. His breath made little clouds as he exhaled, same as hers. "I don't know," he said again. "Maybe no one does." He dropped his gaze and looked at her. "Why haven't you done it before?"

She smoothed his hair out of his eyes and again he let her, but his hair felt cold, sticky. Stiffened with something dark and viscous. "Because I was afraid you'd disappear."

He nodded. "I was, too. That's why I told you to stay up there. So, why'd you come tonight?"

She took a deep breath. "Because you're already disappearing, aren't you?"

He didn't answer, not at first. Then after a minute, he raised one shoulder and dropped his gaze. "I think so. That's what it feels like."

He sounded so sad, so lost, and it broke her heart. She touched his hair again, ignoring the unpleasant texture.

"Okay, then. What do we do about it?"

He gave vent to a frustrated laugh. "I don't know, Mom. I just got done telling you I don't know how it works. I don't even know how I got here in the first place." His eyes met hers. "Do you?"

She considered not telling him. He'd always been so protective of her, and she worried that he'd tell her to stop if he knew what she was doing. She hedged. "I've been making a...sacrifice, I guess you could say."

His brows went up, and he took a step away from her. "Like, of the animal kind? Jesus, Mom." His eyes went wide. "Not Penny Lane?"

She laughed, that strange little niggle of doubt silenced by his use of the cat's name. "Of course not. No animals were harmed in the making of this visit."

He grinned. "Okay, good. So then, more like a personal sacrifice, right?"

The nicks and cuts that patterned her skin put up a throb of protest. "Exactly."

"So has anything been different about it? Anything changed?"

She shook her head. She was never haphazard about the amount of blood she spilled— she'd worried that there was a precise measurement she had to meet, or she would miss seeing her son; her sacrifice wasted. "Nothing's changed that I know of."

He shrugged again. "Then maybe it has to be more."

She frowned. "More, what?"

"More quantity? Or more quality? Maybe the nature of it has to increase, if we want to keep going. Maybe," he said, leaning in close, "whatever you're giving up has to be worth more to be effective."

She watched him, feeling the blood drain from her face, glad it was so dark. "You think so?"

He laughed. "Hell, I don't know, Mom. All I know..." his voice trailed off, and the smile dropped. "All I know is how I feel. Which is tired, and... I don't know. Faded or something. It's getting worse."

Chris could tell. She knew she hadn't been wrong in discerning there was something off with her son. She took a breath. "Okay. You could be right; I'll work on it. Make some tweaks. In the meantime..." she stopped, afraid of rejection in a way she never had been with Trey. He seemed fragile, though, or maybe brittle was the word she was looking for. As moody and explosive as he'd ever been in the throes of adolescence.

He blew his breath out. "In the meantime, *what?*"

"In the meantime, would you like to come inside? Get warm?"

He shook his head. "I can't, Mom. I don't even know what warm feels like, anymore."

She could tell he was getting ready to leave her again. She reached up to the full extent of her five-foot-two-inch frame and threw her arms around his neck, drawing him close. "It feels like this, Trey," she said into his ear when he leaned down to put his head on her shoulder.

He sighed, and it sounded like crying. She patted his back and kissed his cheek, and didn't think about the way he smelled, like something past its expiration date, or the way her lips felt greasy after touching his skin. She just held him, and she would have stayed like that until she died, if he'd let her. But he pulled away far too soon, and she was left standing in the cold, her arms bereft, watching him go. Wondering how to make it right, how to give more than she already was. Wondering how much of her it would take.

CHAPTER NINE

Chris was apprehensive the whole next day, waiting to visit the cross. She was afraid in a way she hadn't been previously—afraid of what was being asked of her. She had a high pain tolerance, and she wasn't squeamish, but it hadn't taken her long to determine that if an increased quantity of blood didn't do the trick, things were going to get gruesome.

She'd canceled with Dan, citing an armful of case files she would be bringing home with her. He'd acquiesced without protest, which made her feel guilty. He'd been the one to make all the concessions so far, hadn't asked her for anything in return, and she knew it was because he was afraid to scare her off. It was pleasant, and easy, in some ways, to let him cater to her wants and never explain herself, but it wasn't sustainable in the long run. It wasn't even desirable. She didn't want to perpetuate that kind of unevenness, nor did she want to hide forever behind the persona of broken mother who always needed to get her way. If she were honest, there were times she would have liked to stay the night with Dan, to wake up in his bed, to do what he wanted on a Saturday.

Parenting came with sacrifice, though, and as she sat on the frozen ground at the base of Trey's cross, shivering and trying to get up the nerve to make the next cut, she knew she was lucky to even have a chance to make those sacrifices.

She'd brought a straight razor with her this time. Before, she'd always made do with a kitchen knife, or in a few instances, a pair of scissors. If she wanted to increase her supply, though, she was going to have to do better.

Razors had always creeped her out a little, ever since she'd first snuck and borrowed her mother's when she was thirteen. Lenora hadn't wanted her to start shaving until she was fifteen, but most of the other girls were already doing it, and gym class was starting to get hellish. The house only had one bathtub, and the razor always stayed on the edge, next to the shampoo and bubble bath. Chris had experimented, sliding it down her leg, baring down a bit because it didn't seem to be doing anything. She'd felt a sting, but it hadn't prepared her for the gouts of blood that gushed into the water in the razor's path. She looked back at it, confused, and saw huge chunks of thin-sliced flesh hanging from the blade. Horrified, she'd looked closer and realized she'd half skinned herself without even knowing. It was that sick moment of seeing the injury before she felt it that disturbed Chris, and it still turned her stomach when she caught her ankle from time to time.

They were sure as hell good for blood flow, though, and that was what she needed now. It was near dark already, the days getting short this close to Halloween. She pulled up the cuff of her jeans and looked at her calf, half frozen and already covered with wounds in various states of healing. She took a breath to steel herself, listening for him again, but she heard nothing. She hadn't heard her son's voice in her head since the very first night he appeared, and though she knew what she had now was so much more precious, she missed it. Especially in moments like these when she was scared.

"No one's going to show up and talk you out of it, Chris," she muttered to herself, and gritting her teeth, she sliced the blade across the fleshiest portion.

"Mother*fuck*," she swore, stopping herself at the last second from clapping a hand to the flowing blood. It had hurt like hell, but she'd achieved her object: her blood was pooling on the frozen ground. She glanced behind her, staring into the dark growth that bordered this little cleared out spot. She could have sworn she heard something, a moan almost, at the exact time the blade bit into her flesh. She didn't see anything, but she had an uneasy feeling of being watched. She remembered all the buried items, and how they'd gone missing. Shit. Was someone here, watching her?

The sun had sunk out of sight by now, and it was full dark in Chris's hollow by the cross. The temperature had dropped, and her bare leg burned on one side, frozen on the other. She looked down again and for a moment was shocked by the amount of blood that had gathered. It made a thick, black pool, reflecting what little starlight there was. Surely that was enough, if anything could be. The wound showed no signs of stopping, and as she peered closer she could see where the flesh had separated, deeper than she'd meant it to.

"Fuck me," she muttered, and another moan sounded, somewhere close.

Chris froze, listening, searching the darkness. There'd been no mistaking it this time—someone was there, watching her making a blood sacrifice. Whatever they were doing, moaning in the bushes, it couldn't be good for her. She needed to get out of here.

She'd come prepared, bringing one of the high tensile rubber strips she'd been given to help with rehabbing her knee when she'd hurt it a few years before, and used it to tie off her leg, just above the wound. She folded the razor and put it away, then began hobbling up the steep grade, back to her car. She was listening for the sounds of pursuit, but all she heard as she reached the top was another long, mournful moan. It sounded closer, but still she saw no one. How could she? She never once looked up.

CHAPTER TEN

I t took hours for the wound in Chris's leg to stop oozing blood, and she thought there was a good chance she'd need stitches. As she limped through the front door, she was glad she'd had the forethought to cancel her date with Dan. Though she was spooked and would have welcomed a warm and enveloping hug that always smelled of soap and sandalwood, she knew he would have overreacted to her injury.

Still, she was feeling sorry for herself as she eased into the kitchen, until she found the dinner he'd left her on the stove. Even through the aluminum foil she could smell the buttery white wine sauce he used to make chicken piccata, and by the time she'd curled up on the couch with her leg propped on the coffee table, dinner on her lap and a glass of wine at her side, she was feeling close to human.

She'd almost managed to banish the vision she'd had as she first realized she wasn't alone in that lonely clearing. For just a moment, she'd had the clearest image of herself, how crazy she must have looked. How great a chance there was that whoever was lurking nearby wasn't as dangerous as a middle-aged woman who'd convinced herself that in order to see her dead son's ghost, she had to slice herself open with a straight razor and cover the ground with blood. She'd seen herself as if from above, and she'd shrunk from the sight, turning away so she didn't have to see her own desperation.

But now she was home, safe behind locked doors, snug, and waiting for her son. Hoping he'd have felt the effects already, that he might be feeling stronger, able to stay for longer. Maybe even warm. And she knew that no matter how crazy it might seem from the outside, there was nothing she could give that would be too great a sacrifice for that reward.

CHAPTER ELEVEN

C hris woke on the couch in full darkness to a frantic tapping at the back glass. She sat up, fully awake now and in a panic as she squinted to see the clock above the stove. Oh God, past time for Trey to be here, and she lunged to her feet, hissing at the pain in her injured leg. She felt the flesh split open, warm blood flowing down to soak the back of her sock, but she limped along and headed for the back door where something still tapped.

She stood on tiptoes to peer out, then cursed when the flexion made her leg scream. She couldn't see anyone, but the tapping continued. If this were a horror movie, she and Trey would both have been yelling at the screen, telling her not to be so fucking stupid, but it wasn't, so she unlocked and opened the door.

No one was there. *He* wasn't there, which was what she'd been hoping for. Ignoring the cold, she limped into the backyard, then went back through the house and out the front door.

He was waiting for her, beneath the streetlight, and she broke into a gimpy jog.

"Oh hell, baby, I'm sorry, I can't believe I slept through. I must have been more tired than I thought." It was true she was exhausted, but she was always tired, and it had never happened before. Once she reached his side and stopped, she realized how dizzy she was. She put a hand out to steady herself and he took it, his own fingers cold, his flesh paper thin.

"Mom? What's wrong with your leg? What'd you do to yourself?"

"I was trying something," she said, her eyes eager to catch the signs of her success. She wanted him to look brighter, happier, stronger than he had been, but he was thinner than ever, his color fading to an insubstantial gray. "Did it help?" she asked, though her heart was sinking. She knew the answer before he spoke it.

He hunched a shoulder, his smile weak. "Maybe it takes time?"

She smiled back, as she was used to doing for him, no matter how she felt. "Maybe so. But if I need to make more adjustments, I will."

He frowned. "I should've asked, before, what you meant by sacrifice—is it physical? I don't want you hurting yourself for me."

She could have told him that motherhood was one long road of pain shouldered whenever it was possible, but she didn't say things like that because she believed in smiling sacrifice. Her mother had never let her forget what Chris owed her, how it was her responsibility to make up for a lifetime of trauma and rejection. No sacrifice Lenora made was without price, all of it to be paid by her daughter. Chris didn't feel that way—to her way of thinking, sacrifice went one way, and laying on the guilt wasn't part of it.

She patted his cold, greasy cheek, moved aside his lank and sticky hair. "It's nothing for you to worry about, kiddo. I'm just glad I get to see you, be close to you. I've missed you." She stumbled over those last words, bringing her face to face with the knowledge, again, that he was gone.

"Missed you, too, Mom." He bent close for another hug, and it was like hugging a scarecrow. He felt as insubstantial as when he'd been a newborn, so lightweight she thought she might misplace him.

He was gone soon after, his shortest visit yet. She stayed out on the street watching after him, as she always did. She didn't know where he went when he left her, didn't know how long he might be able to look back and see her. When she turned to limp back inside, she thought she saw movement behind Dan's front window but was too tired to care. Let him make of it what he would. She had other problems to solve.

CHAPTER TWELVE

Chris had passed out again after Trey left, and it only occurred to her the next morning, when she woke with a headache, to wonder if it had anything to do with the amount of blood she'd lost. Clearly that wasn't sustainable, nor was it even useful—she'd opened herself up with that razor for nothing. Whatever she might say to Trey, she didn't believe that her sacrifices had a delayed effect. Each time she'd gotten it right, he'd come the same night.

After a short debate, she ended up calling in to work. She ignored the harried tone of her supervisor, making passive aggressive attempts to get her to reconsider. She never called in, and this was important. And if the woman was honest, she knew that the job needed Chris much more than Chris needed the job.

She turned her phone off after that, and spent the day thinking, deciding, and once her decision was made, psyching herself up for the task. Girding her loins, she thought the expression went, and it had never seemed so apt. The idea of what she was planning to do sent shivers through her gut and down to her genitals, much the way that certain things had made Beau's balls shrivel up, as he phrased it.

She would have liked to get a nice buzz before she did it, but she damn sure wasn't going to drink and drive, which left out getting hammered at the cross as well. She supposed she could stay long enough to let it wear off, but the memory of the watcher made her want to get in and out as soon as possible. She hated that feeling. Going to the cross had used to bring her peace, had brought her closer to her son. There'd been occasions she'd spent hours at a time out there, bringing a picnic lunch with all Trey's favorites, spending time with him. She was angry at whoever had invaded her sacred place and robbed her of her peace.

But if she were being honest, she'd been feeling apprehensive long before the previous night. As much as it excited her to get home after an offering, and know she'd be getting a visit that night in return, it was unnerving knowing what she had to do first. She'd grown weary of the pain, and now she was even more so. Blood wasn't enough; she would have to bury more of herself out there.

It had taken some thought, to decide where to start. There were amputations, as an obvious first step. Fingers and toes, but there were only ten of each, not an unlimited supply. Things like that didn't grow back; they didn't replicate the way blood cells did. Once she cut off a toe, that would be it, no going back. And she wasn't stupid—she knew even a pinky toe could affect her balance, her ability to walk unassisted. Fingers would be even worse—she pictured trying to drive to the cross with nothing but stumps above her palms. It was a horrible thought, but it also made sense—this was all about sacrifice, and giving up something she knew would come back, like the blood, simply wasn't enough anymore.

In the end, she decided on skin. The idea was no less horrible—though the scars would eventually heal, it wouldn't be fast, and she'd never be the same. She'd gotten the idea from a bleak, dystopian horror novel she'd read years ago. *Ration* had been set in a dark future in which girls and women were all that were left, and only worth as much as the calories their bodies could provide to those with more power and money. One of the characters, banished to the street, had chosen to sell strips of her skin to survive. Chris had understood her reasoning at the time, though she'd shrunk from the idea of it. If making a single incision with a razor hurt that much, how the hell was she going to make herself remove an entire patch of skin? And even if she could, how much would be enough to satisfy whatever dark god had given her this chance?

She couldn't do much without alerting Dan that something was very wrong, but that was part of the cost. What was more important, her boyfriend or her son? She silenced the part of her mind that asked why there had to be a choice.

Dan might have to go, she knew, and it broke her heart to think it, but she wouldn't draw back. She wouldn't leave her boy alone out there, only half manifested, growing more tired and faded by the day. And it *was* her boy, she told herself, stomping the doubt that wanted to wriggle in and steal her resolve. So, in full dark that night, she sat cross-legged in the dirt, freezing in a long and airy skirt. She was going to start with her legs, because she'd be able to use both hands, and it would be easier to see what she was doing.

Still worried about the intruder of the previous night, she'd brought her gun with her this time and made a full perimeter check before the sun fell. She found no one, and no sign that anyone had been there recently. There were old beer cans and discarded fast food wrappers, but nothing recent, and the plant growth was undisturbed.

Now the gun was lying beside her, a 9mm semi-auto she sometimes carried with her for more isolated claims adjusting trips. She'd gone to the range a great deal back when Trey was a trying teenager—it was good stress relief, but she hadn't fired a gun in years.

She'd set up a large flashlight on an empty copy paper box she'd brought from work, a makeshift operating theater. Her heart pounded. Sweat poured from her hands and she had to keep wiping them to keep the blade from slipping. She was using the same straight razor as the night before, and she dreaded its whisper-sharp touch.

Nothing for it but to do it, she told herself, tracing the small, square outline she'd drawn on her thigh with a black sharpie. She gritted her teeth, held her breath, and sliced. Whatever sounds might have been issued from other throats were drowned out by her screams.

CHAPTER THIRTEEN

Another night of waiting, while trying to kill the pain. Another night of putting off Dan, when all she wanted was to find comfort in his arms. She'd texted him instead of calling because she didn't think she could hear his voice without breaking down. It wasn't just that she knew she was hurting him, although that bothered her, a lot. It was the trauma. She remembered, in the days and weeks after her hellish two-day labor with Trey, how the slightest thing had made her burst into tears at the memory of it, at the horror of what she'd been through. Nothing could have prepared her for that kind of pain, and it left its mark on her for years afterward.

It was the same principle here, she told herself, huddled on the couch in the dark, old episodes of *Law & Order* on for company. She hadn't felt like eating, but the generous bourbon she'd poured herself was making inroads on the pain and taking the edge off her mental state. She didn't want to get plastered and risk sleeping through her time with Trey again, but she needed something to dull the agony. She kept seeing it, the blade scraping up under the patch of sacrificial skin. She squeezed her eyes shut against it and refilled her glass, not even bothering with ice this time.

She'd put her phone alarm on its loudest setting for ten minutes before Trey's usual arrival time, so this time she was the one waiting for him under the streetlight. As soon as he showed, her stomach dipped. It hadn't worked, hadn't been enough. He was thinner and grayer than ever, his eyes sunk deep into a face that looked more like a skull by now.

She could have cried. She almost did, feeling the throb of twin injuries—the slice on her calf that still hadn't closed, and that raw patch on her thigh of exposed *something*—what did you call that second layer, was it just more skin? Was it muscle? She hadn't been able to make herself look at it, and it was covered now by a loose gauze bandage. The night's bitter cold stung them both.

Trey looked sad, and unapproachable. He didn't take his hands from his pockets, making it hard for her to get her arms around him, but she more or less muscled him into the hug, as she had in the tumultuous days of adolescence when he'd tried to freeze her out with his anger. It was like hugging smoke, and she fought the urge to tighten her grip. It would only make him slip through her fingers.

"Guess it didn't work," he said when she allowed him to pull away. His voice was hollow and dull, and sounded less than ever like her boy.

"I guess it didn't," she said, with as much of a lift to her voice as she could manage. She was tired, and she was hurting, but as ever, that wasn't his burden to bear.

He sighed, and slumped to the ground, resting on the curb, his long legs bent, forehead resting on his knees. "I'm so tired, Mom."

Biting her lip against the agony it caused her, she lowered herself to sit next to him, a hand on his insubstantial back. "I know you are, baby. I'm working on it, I promise."

He pulled into himself, away from her touch. "What're we going to do? How do I get out of this? Am I just going to fade away until I'm...gone, again?"

The fear in his voice made her stomach knot. She didn't know where he went when he wasn't with her, but if he was afraid of it, she wouldn't let him go back. "I'll fix it, Trey. I tried something, I thought it would be enough, but it wasn't. That's okay, I'm not out of ideas. We're not beat yet, okay, kiddo?"

His shoulders shook; he wiped a sleeve across his face. He was crying. "I'm just so tired. I'm so cold, and scared, and I don't even know where I am most of the time. I hate this."

Dread filled her heart. In spite of her faith, her lifelong belief that there was something beyond this life, she'd always been afraid that there was nothing but a cold, black void awaiting all of them. And now, the fear that her son wouldn't be waiting for her when she crossed over; that death would never bring him any closer than he was right now, was stronger than ever. She wanted to ask him what it was like, what he remembered, but she was scared.

She laid her head on his shoulder, one hand still moving in a soothing circle on his back. "I wish I could take it from you, baby. I wish I could wave a wand and make it mine."

It was an old wish, repeated often ever since the very first virus Trey had come down with as a baby. As her helpless four-month-old had doubled up in pain, vomiting over and over, she had begged to take his suffering on as her own. She'd meant it, every time she'd said it, as she meant it now.

"I wish you could, too," he said, then went quiet. He said nothing else in the short, precious time they had together, and this time, he didn't stand and walk away into the shadows. Instead, he was simply gone, and she was left with her hands around empty air.

She wept bitterly when she got back inside, both her legs in agony now that the bourbon had worn off. She knew she wouldn't sleep like this and was wondering what the hell to do with herself for the next few hours until sunrise, when a light tapping sounded at her kitchen door. She went to it, heart thudding, remembering the night Trey had tapped to wake her. But when she opened it and saw Dan standing there, shirtless under his unzipped winter coat, the fear she'd felt evaporated. She hated herself for feeling that way, but the knowledge of what she'd have to do come daylight had filled her heart with dread.

He didn't step over the threshold until she threw herself in his arms. Then he crushed her to him, her wet cheek against his bare chest, and moved them both inside, out of the cold. He stood and held her in the dark while she cried, wrapping his coat around her, and not saying a word. When she finally moved away, he saw the way she limped, and he picked her up and carried her to the couch.

It was a strange feeling. Chris had never thought of herself as the type of woman who could be carried—she was no lightweight, even when she was young, but Dan lifted her with ease and settled in with her on his lap, her head on his shoulder, careful of her bandaged calf.

"I'm not gonna ask you what happened," he said after a few minutes. "You can tell me if you want, and I'll listen, but I don't expect you plan to tell me the truth about that leg, any more than you have about all the other injuries. All I want to know is if there's anywhere else I should be careful of."

He said it without rancor, and she started crying all over again. Where had this love been, this unselfish faith and care, when it would have made a difference?

"My thigh," she said when she could speak, hovering one hand over the spot without touching it. Her nightgown was stained dark there where the blood had oozed through the bandage.

"Can I see it?"

She nodded, and he clicked on the living room lamp, lifted the gown with infinite care, and frowned at the soaked bandage.

"We need to change that." He went rummaging through the bathroom, came back with hydrogen peroxide, fresh gauze, and antibacterial ointment. The tube was long expired, left over from Trey's short-lived love affair with skateboarding.

Chris turned her head while he worked, biting her lip so hard it bled. He had to have known, looking at that square patch with regular, straight cut edges, that it had been intentional, but still he didn't ask. When he was finished, he brought her Tylenol and more bourbon, and settled next to her on the couch.

She sipped her drink and waited for him to demand answers. In his place she would have, and she knew he was owed them. She was wondering what she could tell him when he broke the silence.

"Somethin' I've noticed about you, babe, is you don't have a clue how to ask for help when you need it. I get that—lotta women are like that, and maybe it's because they've gotta be." He urged her head down on his shoulder, ran his hand lightly over her uninjured thigh. "That's okay by me. You don't want to talk about what's going on, that's your business. I don't need to know, though I'd be lying if I said I didn't *want* to know. Point is, I don't have to be in the loop to be able to help you, okay? So will you let me?"

It hurt. Jesus, it hurt so much, hearing those words years after she had needed them. They'd never come from Beau because he hadn't understood her, or maybe he hadn't cared enough. He'd loved her, and claimed that he still did, but she'd come to understand it was a selfish love, that he had limits beyond which he wouldn't stretch, not even when she needed him the most.

Dan was right; she really didn't know how to ask for help.

Even now, with the offer open and unfettered, she didn't know what to ask for. How could he help her? He was handy, but there was no trade school for tinkering with death. He needed an answer, but she didn't know how to begin. And in the end, she settled for honesty.

"Yes. If I ever figure out a way you can help me, then yes, I will ask you."

"Okay, sweetheart. I'll just be waiting here until you do."

CHAPTER FOURTEEN

The cross again. The dark, and the cold. Moonlight on the blade, fear making her breath come quick, her hands shake.

This time it wasn't silent. A bitter wind whipped her hair, moved the bare branches to rub against one another, to whisper above the creaks of the heavy limbs above her. Beneath all of it, the undercurrent of those moans.

They'd started the moment she took her first step down the steep grade, and they hadn't let up since. She'd limped the perimeter again, gun in hand, but found no one, and the October branches stripped of leaves left little room for hiding. There was no one to make the moaning, so Chris decided not to hear it.

She had a cleaver this time, a sharp one, honed that afternoon in Dan's workshop. It was sick that she'd even asked him, and she knew it, but he'd wanted to help, so she'd let him. He'd looked ill when he handed it to her, no doubt wanting to take back his rash words. Beau would have, she knew. Beau would have decided what was best for her and supplanted her judgment with his own. Maybe he'd have been right to do so—objectively, Chris knew that what she was doing looked insane, not to mention cruel. Asking her boyfriend to get her a knife sharp enough to amputate a finger—it wasn't the action of a sane woman. And maybe she wasn't one. She didn't feel crazy, and when she ran through the scenario in her mind, this felt like the logical next step. She supposed crazy people never thought they were, wasn't that what people always said? It didn't matter. It wasn't like she was going to check herself in for a psych eval. Either Trey had truly visited her because of the sacrifices she made, and now needed her to go the extra mile, or she was insane, and he was never there at all. And if she had a choice in which reality to stay in, she wanted to be here, with him.

She had a candle lighter she'd found buried in a kitchen drawer and was running it over the blade. She didn't know how much it would help, but she'd always heard a heated blade cut better, and she wanted this to be quick. Not painless, there was no chance of that, but she was afraid she wouldn't be able to keep going, if the first cut didn't do it.

She'd decided on a finger instead of a toe, in spite of her first instinct. Toes were smaller and less visible. You didn't look down hundreds of times a day and see your toes, not unless you were barefoot, so initially a toe seemed less traumatic. But as she considered, as coldly as she could, the mechanics of what she would need to do, she realized a finger was the better choice. It wouldn't affect her balance, and it would be easier to protect. A missing toe would be agony each time she took a step, but she could bandage her hand, put the arm in a sling and keep from using it until the wound healed. Besides, she wasn't sure she'd be able to make herself look while she brought the knife down, and there was too much chance of collateral damage on a foot, with the toes so close together. A pinky finger could be spread, far apart from the other tender digits as they waited their turn to go under the knife.

Deciding the blade must be hot enough by now, she flicked off the flame, and the moaning grew louder. The wind picked up, cutting through her heavy coat and the layers beneath. The branches above her creaked and cracked, and she wondered if there were dead limbs above that might give under the strain, come crashing down to pummel her into the ground, and render all of this effort moot. She searched the darkness overhead, but only saw moving shadows, nothing to tell her if imminent death loomed above. Either way, she'd be better off getting on with it, and getting back home.

She laid her left hand on the block of wood she'd brought with her and looked down at her splayed fingers. She wondered now, considering the angles, whether the thumb would be the easier choice, but she didn't want to give that one up. Not yet. It seemed solid, an anchor, and she'd leave it for last.

She breathed, each time preparing herself for the chop, each time letting it out without bringing the knife down. There were several false starts, when she pulled her hand away at the last second, and she had to stop and heat the blade again. The wind was a scream now, the branches overhead thrashing so hard as to defy belief.

She was hyperventilating, and sweating, and her arms felt like lead. What was she doing? How could she make herself cut off a damn finger to bury in the ground, as a sacrifice to who knew what? Maybe she couldn't do it. Maybe this was too hard, a bridge too far, and she should go home and deal with her loss, the way she should have from the beginning.

Then she thought of the time they'd had to take Trey to the ER when he was only six months old. A bulging fontanel, which seemed odd to her—she'd known that a sunken one meant de-hydration. The pediatrician had run some blood tests, but when they came back negative, the doctor had come into the waiting room and told Chris in a calm voice that she'd called ahead to the hospital, and that they were on standby to do a spinal tap.

"Oh, Jesus God," she'd said, clutching her baby boy to her chest. Horror fan that she was, she could remember with crystal clarity that scene from *The Exorcist*, and the idea of having to subject her infant son to that almost overwhelmed her. She was panicked, and it had seemed more than she could bear. As she raced him to the hospital, Beau on his way to meet them, she'd decided she wouldn't look. She couldn't, not at that. She'd called her office to let them know she wouldn't be back, her voice rising in hysteria as she spoke to one of her co-workers, a veteran mom herself.

"Chris," came the woman's voice. "You're the mom now, Chris. You have to be the adult. That baby needs you, so you do what has to be done, whatever it is."

It was what she'd needed to hear. The words had dried her up, brought her back down to earth, and she'd been able to handle the entire ordeal, better than Beau, and been the one to calm him down as well. In the end the doctor had opted for a cranial ultrasound, which had pissed Trey off enough as it was, and found a benign skull condition, no sign of the meningitis the pediatrician had feared. The whole time her baby lay screaming on the table, through three failed attempts to attach an IV to his little ankle, Chris had held him, locked eyes, and kept calm. Not because that was how she felt, but because it was what he needed.

Just like now. It didn't matter that Trey was dead, or that even if he were alive, he'd be an adult. He was still *her* baby and always would be. She was the mom, and she had to do what was needed, no matter how terrifying.

"Do it, do it, just fucking do it instead of drawing this shit out, Chris," she hissed. Bringing the knife up once more, she sucked breath through her teeth, and as the blade flew down, she heard the wind change. The low moan began again, an eerie *mmmmmmmm* sound, but just before the blade met flesh, it crescendoed into a single word.

Mmmmmmmmooooooommmmmm….the wind cried. Then a sickening crunch of bone, a white-hot blaze of pain, and Chris's world went black.

CHAPTER FIFTEEN

Dan waited as long as he could before coming after her. He'd known she was going to the cross, and he'd known, when he'd given her that sharply honed knife, that she'd be using it. He'd been sick ever since, but he'd felt obligated to follow through on his offer of help. Now he stood at the sink, staring out the kitchen window, and imagining all the awful things she might be doing with that blade. All the things she'd already done to herself. He'd squeezed his eyes shut against the gory images, and finally given up on waiting for her. It'd been long enough, and if she'd run into trouble, the longer he waited, the worse it would be.

He didn't know whether to be relieved when he saw her car parked there at the shoulder. The night was quiet and cold, and he hoped she'd just lost track of time. As he crested the hill and looked down into the hollow, his heart froze in his chest.

Chris was laid out below, curled on her side, one hand a mass of blood and makeshift bandage. *Finger*, he'd thought as he slid his way down to get to her, strangely glad to have an answer to the tortured question of what she was mutilating. The scene was like an abattoir—the blood-soaked knife he'd sharpened for her, lying close to her uninjured hand, bits of flesh clinging to the blade. The finger itself, stark and shocking there all on its own, severed from the hand it had once belonged to. He gagged, and wondered if he should preserve it somehow, but decided to leave it up to her.

She was pale and unconscious, though she was easily roused when he knelt beside her and said her name in a shaky voice. She'd looked confused at first, then the pain must have hit, and he'd taken her in his arms and tried to warm her while she cried. Shock, he thought. She had to be in shock, didn't she? He needed to take her somewhere; his first aid skills fell far short of amputations. She didn't fight him on it but asked him for a minute's privacy. He gave it to her with guilty relief, not wanting to be witness to what she might do with that finger. He helped her up the incline, and they rode back in silence, the atmosphere in the truck heavy with unasked questions.

CHAPTER SIXTEEN

Chris leaned against the door and thought of how it must have looked to him, coming across her alone in that hollow by her son's cross. It was worse than the day Nat caught her out there. She'd had no chance to clean anything up, to make it look like anything other than exactly what it was. He'd seen her bandaged hand, though she didn't remember binding it herself, and the severed finger beside her. The lighter, and the knife he'd sharpened, and there could have been no question in his mind as to what she'd done. She'd made him turn his back while she buried the finger at the base of the cross, woozy from blood loss and pain. She couldn't stop looking at the place where her finger used to be. She wondered if she ever would.

He took her to the ER without asking, but she supposed he was right to do so. The intern asked her if she'd brought the finger with her, and she shook her head, but felt Dan's eyes on her. Had he seen what she'd done with it? What must he think of her, now?

The ER wait had been long, and by the time Dan got her

home it was past eleven. He sat frowning at his steering wheel while she tried to find the energy to climb out of his truck. Fumbling with the seat belt made her suck in her breath as she jammed her thickly wrapped stump. It was a sickening pain, one of absence, and her stomach churned as she tried not to look at it.

He leaned over to help her, then stayed close, looking into her eyes. "Can I come in?" he asked after a minute.

She nodded. It was the least he deserved. "But...you can't stay, okay?" She felt shitty saying it.

"I know," he said.

He stayed with her while she dozed on the couch, halfway between narcotic induced unconsciousness and traumatized nightmares. She'd never given him a specific time he had to leave, but when he roused her by getting up and kissing her cheek, she saw it was fifteen minutes before Trey-o'clock.

She was exhausted and tempted to stay on the couch, but she knew she needed to get up and moving. The wounds on her legs were still burning, the raw skinless patch on her thigh tight with hardened blood under the bandage. It took several minutes to limp out under the streetlamp, but he wasn't there when she arrived.

He wasn't there twenty minutes later, either, and by then Chris's entire body was numb. He'd never been this late before; what if he didn't come at all? What if she'd wasted her window to find the solution, and they'd already had their last meeting?

When he did show, it was as though he'd been dumped there, dropped out the side of some moving cosmic vehicle. He landed with a cry, and stayed there, crumpled on his side.

Chris ran to him as best she could and tried to help him up, jamming her stump again in the process. He was crying and it took effort to get him upright. His face was thin, dirty, and smeared with blood over recent abrasions. His hands were the same, his flesh grayer than ever.

"Mom," he sobbed into her chest, and she was struck with the memory of what had happened at his cross. That mournful moan that had called for her, or at least that was what it had sounded like as she passed into blackness. She shuddered, closed her eyes, and concentrated on her son.

"What happened to you, baby?" she asked as she rocked him.

"I don't know. I don't know, I don't know," he repeated, his voice rising. "It's not right, whatever you're doing isn't right, and it's angry."

Chris's flesh grew even colder. "What's angry, baby? What are you talking about?"

"Whatever brought me here. Whatever you called to, made a bargain with, it's the one controlling me, controlling this, and it's so, so angry."

Her breath was coming quicker, her exhaustion and stupor pushed out of the way by fear and cold. She hadn't called anyone, hadn't made any bargains. It was true, she'd gotten the idea to try bringing Trey back to her from that episode of *Paranormal Warriors*, about the crossroads demon, but that was just a television show, and anyway she hadn't done that. She'd only made offerings. "I thought you said you didn't know who made the rules, Trey?"

He gave a hysterical laugh. "I don't. I didn't, but I know that something is very angry now, and it's taking it out on me."

"Trey, I'm trying. You have to believe me—the sacrifices I've made trying to make this right, they were big. I haven't taken any of this lightly."

"It's not enough!" he screamed, pushing to his feet, Chris falling on her side. "You're not doing enough," he said, tears trickling down his nose. "You've always said, if you could take my suffering and make it your own, you would. So why don't you do that?"

She stared up at him, at his angry, twisted face. Every part of her hurt, and for no benefit. He hadn't even asked about her hand, and his ingratitude was overwhelming.

No. Chris stopped herself. She wasn't going down that road, wasn't going to become her mother. Always railing about what Chris owed to her, for the sacrifices she'd made. Furious at her daughter for the slightest transgression, and always falling back on her ingratitude theme. If Chris were truly grateful for the clothes on her back, the food in her belly, then she wouldn't make mistakes. She heard Lenora's voice in her head, in the words she'd almost said to her son.

She choked them back and thought about what he was asking. Studied his drawn face, the jut of his shoulder blades and clavicle. He was hurting, and looking to her to fix it, so she would.

"Okay, Trey. If that's what it's going to take, I'll do it." Her face and hands were so cold, her voice sounding like something separate from herself.

He only nodded. "Can you hurry, Mom? I don't know how much longer I can take this."

She took a deep breath that hurt her lungs and pushed herself off the curb. "I will. You need to give me a few days to put things in order, but then I'll come, okay?"

An impatient twist of his mouth, but he agreed. As he walked away from her that night, traveling into the shadows under his own steam again, she saw with relief, he turned back to throw one final word over his shoulder. She didn't hear it, but she could read his lips.

Hurry.

CHAPTER SEVENTEEN

She slept a deep and dreamless sleep for the remainder of the night, waking the next morning with a strange sense of calm. It was an oppressive calm, but she'd take her peace however she could get it. She made her slow and painful way down the stairs to make coffee, opting this time to break out the big guns. Whole bean, red velvet, dark roast in the freezer, the kind of thing she reserved for special occasions. There was no point now in saving it.

She sat at her table and looked out into the backyard, lit by an uncertain sun. There was no question of what Chris was being asked to do. If she wanted her son to live, to escape from the hell she'd inadvertently delivered him into, she'd need to give her life for him. Maybe even her soul.

She wanted to scream against the unfairness of it. She hadn't summoned any demon, or made any promises, she was sure of that. All she'd done was try to guess the pattern that she'd found by accident and taken advantage of it. But as she knew from years of claims adjusting, of accident investigations, of cleaning up the aftermath of people's terrible decisions, or plain shitty luck, intention didn't always matter. Whatever had answered her call, her pained and delirious begging for her son to return to her, it had hold of Trey now, and there was only one way to free him.

A few months ago, she'd have jumped at the chance without a second thought. She'd asked for a few days, but in truth, the only thing she needed to sort out was where Penny Lane would go. She thought of Beau, but Natalie had an allergy. It might have to be Dan, though she shrunk from adding one more burden to his overloaded shoulders.

It was Dan she needed the extra time for. Him, and to say goodbye to Beau and Natalie, and the girls. Her mind lighted on her mother, but she dismissed the thought. If she only had a few days left, she didn't want to spend a single second of it listening to Lenora's endless complaints and attempts to get under her daughter's skin. Chris didn't love her mother, and she wouldn't miss her. A terrible thing to admit, and a truth she'd shied away from for years, until the right therapist had pointed out that the woman had done a stellar job of killing any natural love Chris might have held for her.

She wasn't going to spend any time at work, either. She could call in, she knew, and listen to the same harried, passive aggressive guilt trip she always got, no matter how ill she was. Nope, that was yet another thing that wasn't going to get her time. She just wouldn't show or answer her phone. It wasn't like she was going to need the reference.

She spent a pleasant half hour listing out the things she wouldn't waste any time on, before detailing a much smaller list of what she needed to do. It wasn't a task list, but a people list— the ones she needed to tell goodbye. It made her sad, staring down at those names, knowing she wouldn't see them again, but she was uplifted by the absence of her son on that list. This was for Trey. It was all for Trey, and she would have traded the entire human race for his well-being.

She showered and dressed in her most comfortable clothes—the leggings that held everything in just right, eased over her injuries with care, and the long-sleeved, off the shoulder t-shirt that made her feel pretty. She did her makeup, but before she could make it back downstairs the doorbell rang. She ran to it, wondering if Dan had saved her the trouble of a walk next door, but it was Beau on the other side, looking like ten pounds of shit in a five-pound bag.

"Beau? What the hell is wrong with you?"

He was leaning against the doorjamb like he'd fall over without its support. His eyes were red and ringed in dark circles, his face unshaven. He looked like he'd slept in his work clothes.

"I need to talk to you. Can I come in?"

Her gaze went to Dan's window, but the sunlight made it impossible to see if he was there. It occurred to her that he might suspect her of being unfaithful, since she never let him spend the night, and she didn't want to end things with that suspicion. But she couldn't very well kick Beau out on his ass, not when he was so clearly in trouble.

"Come on. Have a seat at the table, the coffee's still hot."

"Smells good," he said as he trailed after her. "Are you limping?"

"It's nothing, I'm fine."

Once they were seated across from one another, he just sat with his hands around his mug, staring down at the maple wood table they'd bought together for their first home.

When several minutes went by in silence, she nudged him. "What did you need to talk to me about, Beau? You look upset. Is everything okay with Nat? With the girls?"

He took a deep, hitching breath. "They're fine. Nat's worried, but she can't help me." He raised his eyes. "It's Trey."

Chris tightened her grip on her own mug, her missing pinky

out of sight. "What about him?"

He let out a vodka-scented breath and her concern deepened. Beau liked a drink as much as the next person, but he'd never been a morning drinker.

"I've been seeing him."

Chris froze, her mind shuffling through the implications. Had Trey been to see Beau? Had Chris's sacrifices benefited her ex-husband, as well? She tamped down on the feeling of annoyance, as though he'd been horning in on her visitation time. Maybe Beau had made his own sacrifices for his son, ones she'd never seen or recognized in her constant state of annoyance.

"What do you mean, you've been seeing him?"

"In dreams," he answered, and she was filled with equal parts relief and disappointment. There had been a short, shameful moment when she'd wondered if it didn't have to be her that traded. Maybe it could be Beau who gave his life, leaving her free to enjoy her son and her boyfriend and the life that had only just recently become worth living again.

"I dream about him, too," she said in a soft voice, but realized that she hadn't in a long time, not since the first visitation.

He shook his head. "Not like that. I mean, I do that too, just see him sometimes. A few nights, especially right after he died, I'd swear it was really him, coming to talk to me in my dreams."

Chris nodded, tears spilling down her cheeks, making tracks in her foundation. She'd had those, too. She'd thought of them as a precursor to his imaginary return to her, that unexamined game she'd played for over a year where she'd pretended he'd never left. She missed those days, those conversations.

"This wasn't like that. There's something wrong, and he's been trying to tell me what it is."

She frowned. "How do you mean? What's he saying is wrong?"

He shook his head, rasped a dry hand across his stubble. "That's just it; I don't know. I can't make it out. He can't speak clearly to me, and I haven't been able to find a way to understand it. He's upset, though, really upset. He's angry that I can't work it out, and it feels like time is running out. I can't sleep, I keep waking up yelling. And I feel like shit, because..."

He trailed off, dropped his gaze. "It's gotten to the point that I don't want to fall asleep, because I don't want to see him. Not like that."

"Like what, Beau? Tell me what you see, what he's saying. Maybe I can help." It had always been that way when Trey was little. Beau had never been able to decipher the toddler's babbling, but Chris had known his language.

Tears were dripping from the end of his nose; he wiped the back of his hand against them. "He's dead, Chris. In every dream he's dead."

She winced. Even in dream speak, she didn't like to think of it. It doesn't matter, she told herself. In a very short time, none of this will matter.

"What do you mean by that, that he's dead in your dreams? You mean you know, even while you're dreaming, that he's gone?"

"No. I mean he...he looks dead. And not just still or anything, he looks like..." he swallowed, choked, and she wasn't sure he'd be able to finish. "He looks like he did, coming out of that tree."

It was a punch to the gut. The image she'd tried her hardest to keep out of her head when she thought of her son. They'd both been there to witness it, through some accident of fate and god-awful timing. They'd gotten their respective calls, both driven out to the site of Trey's wrecked vehicle believing that he must have walked away, dazed, and needed their help to come home. Beau had gotten there first, and she'd been looking at him while he'd been looking up, hands clamped over his mouth, a muffled moaning escaping from behind his fingers.

She'd gotten to his side, put an arm around him and opened her mouth to ask what was wrong, but the words died on her lips when she'd followed his gaze up into the oak tree that towered above.

It was only then that she'd seen the ladder extended from the firetruck, emergency personnel high up in the tree, the bright, reflective stripes on their uniforms making them easy to see through the green branches. It took longer for her to pick out Trey up there, his jeans and dark t-shirt blending in, as though in death, his body had melded with the tree somehow.

Watching the EMTs hand her son down in slow, tender movements, her heart surged, then felt as though it cracked down the middle. She'd wanted to hope. To hold onto the belief that though he might be badly hurt, he'd have a chance. A long road to recovery, but she'd be there for him, and they'd get him back on his feet. It was what they told cancer patients, and women struggling with infertility—just fight, stay positive, hang onto the hope. An insidious claim, given the other edge of the blade—if you lost hope, if you plunged into negativity, had you doomed yourself? Had Chris doomed Trey's chance of survival when she saw the way his head lolled, the limp movements of his arms and legs, the crushed-in state of his skull? Had he truly only died in that exact moment when his mother lost faith?

She'd known, once he was out of the tree, strapped to a stretcher though he moved no more, that it was an image she'd never be able to get out of her head. His ruined skull, brain and blood and bits of bone sticking up amongst the sticky clumps of hair. The unnatural angle of his neck. It was what she would always see when she thought of her boy, unless she could do something drastic to replace it.

So she had. Pictured, dreamed, imagined into being the Trey she had always known, the boy she'd raised, one day at a time, until that was all she saw. But that other image of Trey as he'd been in death had been waiting, and at Beau's words it reared its head, and smothered her memories.

"I don't know what to say, Beau. That's a terrible nightmare to have."

He shook his head. "Not a nightmare. That's what I'm trying to tell you—I think he appeared that way to me because he had no choice. It's got to take effort, don't you think? To show up in our dreams looking hunky-dory? And maybe this time the message was too urgent, and he didn't have any energy reserves to make it pleasant viewing."

Chris could only look at him. What he was saying made a certain kind of sense, but it didn't line up with her recent experiences. Why would Trey appear to her in person, looking, at least at first, just like his old self, only to appear in broken form in his father's dreams? She was loath to tell Beau what she suspected, that despite its lucid and urgent nature, it was still only a dream, but it was the only answer that made sense.

"You said he was trying to tell you something. Do you remember anything he said?" she asked.

Beau hunched one shoulder. "It's not a matter of remembering—I remember every second, which is another reason I know these dreams are different. They don't fade when I wake up because he was really there. It's that I can't understand the message, like he's too far away. I mean, he's right next to me in the dream, but it's like he's underwater, or, I don't know, behind some kind of invisible screen. He gets kind of blurry and agitated, but all I can make out are muffled words that don't make sense." He took her hand, the one with all fingers intact, thankfully, and pressed it tight. "The only thing I know for sure is that whatever he wants to tell me, it's about you."

She frowned at him, more confused than ever. "How do you know that?" She thought again of that strange, muffled moan of the night before that had sounded just like someone calling "mom." Was that what Beau had heard in his dreams?

He smiled enough to make his tears take a detour. "He uses

sign language. Remember, the baby sign language they used to teach them in daycare?"

She did. Trey had been independent from birth, frustrated at his limitations even as an infant, and once he learned to sign a few words—"more," "milk," and "mom," mostly—he'd been thrilled. He never learned much more than that, but they had all retained the memory of those three signs.

"He signed for me?" she asked in a small voice.

Beau nodded, pressed her hand tighter. "That's why I needed to come see you. I put it off, even after I realized that was what he was saying, because I didn't want to upset you. You've seemed so good lately, even Natalie's noticed." His smile was short-lived, but genuine. "Love suits you, Chris."

Her lip trembled, thinking of Dan; of what she was going to do to him, what she'd already done by pulling him into her quest.

Beau let go of her hand. "Anyway, that was why I didn't say anything at first, but last night..." His eyes were haunted, the exhaustion deepening even as she watched. "Last night he made it pretty clear I didn't have a choice. Whatever it is he's upset about, it has to do with you, and he's not going to give me any peace until I pass it on."

Chris stared at her ex-husband without seeing him, her gaze fixed in the middle distance, her sight turned inward. It didn't make any sense, what he was saying. Didn't line up at all with what had been happening, or what she'd been asked to do. Unless it did...was Trey simply trying to convey to his father how necessary and urgent his need was?

Beau said something and she focused on him again.

"Sorry, what'd you say?"

"I just said, I hope you're being careful. Not planning any plane rides in the near future, or exposing yourself to mass disaster." He was half smiling, but she knew he meant it.

She patted his hand. "I'm taking care of myself, Beau. I always have."

She saw him out, happy that at least he looked less burdened as he drove away, hopefully in the direction of home. But his visit had only added to her burden, as she couldn't understand what it meant in the context of her decision. Trey hadn't looked dead when he appeared to her—even his injuries of the night before were different, not consistent with what had killed him. And she'd seen him, spoken to him, held him only hours before. She'd listened to him, heard his request, and told him she would do it. So why the urgent dream visits to Beau?

It could only mean she'd been right in her first thought—that Beau's visit had been nothing more than a dream, wishful thinking, the same kind of thing she'd woken from so many times in the early days after Trey's death, heartbroken all over again once she remembered he was gone. She could see why he'd been convinced otherwise. There were dreams Chris still remembered, that hadn't faded with the passage of time, that she'd been certain had meant he'd really visited her. She wouldn't take that certainty away from Beau—he'd looked so upset, so lost and helpless. Guilt stabbed her again, thinking of what it would do to him once she carried through on her promise. They weren't married anymore, and she knew Dan would bear the heaviest burden, but Beau still loved her as a friend, as the mother of his son, the woman who had his past. She would have to think about what she could do to soften the blow, and she added it to her to-do list.

CHAPTER EIGHTEEN

The question that loomed the largest was, how to do it? What method would she use to snuff out her own life, and trade it for her son's? Was there only one right way, a specific death that would allow the transfer, or did it not matter as long as the sacrifice was made? She didn't know the answer to that question, or who to ask. That night she waited for Trey to show, though she hadn't made a trip to the cross that day. It hadn't seemed worth it. She had nothing new to offer, not yet, and the thought of being there filled her with dread. It had become a place of pain and trauma, and she didn't want to make things worse for herself.

So she wasn't surprised that he didn't appear that night, though it did seem unfair. Were the sacrifices she'd made so far not enough to at least allow her a glimpse of her son? Not even to get answers to the questions that would make sure her death wasn't in vain? It was a big ask, one that for anyone else would be a bridge too far. Not for Trey, never for Trey, but was it too much to expect a guarantee?

The next morning, she went to Dan's early. He was still in pajamas but didn't look like he'd slept. He took her in his arms, surreptitiously checking her for new injuries.

"I didn't go yesterday, remember?" She'd spent the evening with him and Toots before going back home to wait for Trey, so he knew that already.

He squeezed her closer, resting his chin on her head. "I know. I just worried you might have done it somewhere else."

She took a deep breath. There it was, out in the open. The admission of her self-harm. She pressed her face to his bare chest, breathing deep of his clean scent. "I'm not going to be doing that anymore," she said, the reality of it leaving her breathless. "And I'd like to stay tonight, if that's okay."

He pulled away to look at her, his smile wide. "Really? The whole night, you mean?"

She nodded, returned his smile, but hers was sad and he noticed. He led her to the kitchen table and brought her coffee in her favorite mug.

"There's more to it, isn't there?"

Part of her wanted to brush it off, to kick the can down the road and enjoy these last few days with Dan. She wanted to give him her all, alleviate his worry, and live in the moment. Seeing the hope in his face, she couldn't do it to him. It would be cruel. But the words to make it clear to him, to make him understand what was coming, were suffocated by tears. She hadn't expected letting go to hurt this much.

"I'm...I'll be going away in a few days," was all she managed to say.

He frowned down at his mug. "And will you be coming back?"

She could only shake her head, biting her lips hard to keep from crying.

He kept his eyes on the surface of his coffee, his hands clenching and unclenching on the table. Finally, he nodded and looked up at her. "Is there anything I could say or do to change your mind, Chris?"

Again, she shook her head, and he sighed.

"Okay, then. Just tell me how long we have."

She raised a shoulder. "Two days? Maybe three?"

His jaw muscles bunched, he swallowed. Then he smiled and took her hand. "I can work with that."

CHAPTER NINETEEN

They lived the next days like doomed passengers on the Titanic, the ones in first class. They ate ridiculously expensive and wonderful meals. He brought her chocolate desserts from everywhere he could think of, and they drank themselves silly on all her favorites, though he was careful never to mix it up—he didn't want her to spend any of her remaining time sick. They made love five or six times a day, and she couldn't help giggling at his obvious pride in the feat. Time felt short, growing shorter all the time, but they tried to block it out by concentrating on each other.

Chris still wasn't sure if Dan knew what exactly she was planning. He hadn't said, and neither had she—she was afraid if he did know, he'd feel obligated to stop her. And in his shoes, she knew she'd have done the same. Suicidal thoughts and promises? Of course she'd intervene, make an effort to talk sense into the person, bring them around to an understanding of the value of life. And she knew Dan was the kind of guy who always did the right thing, so she came to the conclusion that he must not understand. She wasn't going to go out of her way to educate him, so her darker plans she made in private.

She was still struggling with the how of it. There were endless ways to take your own life, and problems with all of them. How reliable the method was, how painful, how much mess it would leave to clean up. The biggest worry for Chris, though, was whether it would fit the requirements of whatever entity it was out there pulling her puppet strings.

She'd started thinking of it that way, though she still only half believed it. Was there really an intelligence behind all this, and one malevolent enough to ask for the kinds of sacrifices she'd been making? That would ask for this ultimate sacrifice, just when things were going well for her? And if there were, could she believe it would uphold its end of any bargain they'd struck? Trey had believed it, and borne the marks to prove it, an image that made her heart heavy with guilt. She knew that every day she delayed her trade, was another day he'd be suffering. If she knew for certain that any old suicide would do, she'd have rushed to finish before he could feel another moment of pain.

At least, she hoped that was true. Because if she were honest, the closer it got to her self-imposed deadline, the less she wanted to say goodbye. It wasn't fair, but she knew better than to rail down that road. Life wasn't fair, and no one had ever promised it would be.

She did the best she could, praying each night for wisdom, reading what material she could find on the internet that dealt with blood sacrifice. Each night, in the small hours, she would still wake and stand at Dan's kitchen window, staring at the empty spot under the streetlight, waiting for Trey to appear. He never did.

On the morning of what she'd privately decided would be her last day, she still hadn't reached any conclusions about how to do it. She felt panicky about it, now the time was almost at hand.

She'd fantasized about it so often in the months after Trey's death—every item she saw became a possible weapon of self-harm, but now she just didn't know. What was the right way? There was nothing to tell her, and no one to ask.

She traipsed across the yards that morning, heading for her own place to check the mail and get clean clothes. Penny Lane had made the trip over to Dan's on the first night she'd stayed, at his insistence. She got the feeling he wasn't much of a cat fan, but he was making an effort, and she loved him for it. It made her feel better about leaving Penny with him when she was gone.

Her heart rate kicked up when she turned the knob on the kitchen door and found it unlocked. Someone was here. Trey, perhaps, to ask why she hadn't fulfilled her promise? Or more likely Beau, with his confusing accounts of Trey's dream visits. But neither of these turned out to be the case. When Chris stepped into her kitchen, it was to see her mother rummaging in her medicine cabinet next to the stove. Irritation hit her in the chest, and she slammed the door behind her.

"Can I help you find something?" she asked.

Lenora turned, one hand on her hip, the other clutching a pharmacy bottle with Chris's name on it. Her thin lips were pursed; she didn't seem the least bit disconcerted to be found snooping.

"Don't you know better than to take this stuff, Christine?" She was holding Chris's antidepressants. "It's terrible for you—you're not in your right mind when you're stuffing yourself with chemicals like this."

Chris closed her eyes and counted to five. When she opened them, Lenora was still standing there waiting for an answer.

"What're you doing here, Mom?"

"I *came* to check on my only daughter. Not that I expect any thanks for it, and never mind that at my age, you should be the one checking on me."

Right. Because like everything else that came into Lenora's orbit, Trey's death was ultimately about her. It was her tragedy, and Chris and everyone else were just bit players.

"I'm fine, Mom, thanks for asking. Anything else?"

Her heart sank when her mother settled in at the kitchen table. She didn't have time for this, but even after years of therapy, she didn't know how to do something as simple as kick her own mother out of her house. She saw Lenora's trembling lip, her welling eyes, and she tried to care, but all she felt was resentment.

"I'm just very alone right now, Chris. You haven't been to see me, not even on the anniversary. My friends all asked about it— they couldn't believe my daughter had left me alone on a day like that." She raised her eyes and gave a tremulous smile. "Don't worry, I made your excuses for you, but it wasn't easy."

It made Chris's blood boil, thinking of those simpering old ladies siphoning drama from her mother, letting her slurp up the sympathy, and the attention from Trey's death. She was so angry she could have vomited. Speak your truth, she reminded herself. It's not your job to manage her emotions.

"He was *my* son, Mom. Not yours. Mine. And I have every right to grieve the way I need to, or remember him how I want to, without catering to what you want out of it. I spent the anniversary of his death with Beau and his family, and I talked to you that night when you called. That's more than enough."

Lenora's eyes narrowed and her lips compressed. Her shoulders began to tremble with a familiar rage. Her voice, when she spoke, was tight and rose at intervals with spurts of fury. "You never listened to me. I had a wealth of experience behind me, raised you as a single mother and did a damn fine job. I gave up so much for you—everything I had. I would have died for you, no matter how poorly you treated me. I still would. I did the hard things every day as a parent, and that's something you'll never understand."

Chris laughed, which made her mother's face narrow even further. "I understand sacrifice, Mom. Better than you'll ever know."

Lenora gave the derisive laugh that had used to cut at her daughter when she was little, five or six years old. "I doubt that very much. I told you at the time, didn't I? I knew that car was trouble. As soon as I saw it, I thought to myself, something terrible is going to happen." She closed her eyes and leaned her head back like a clairvoyant.

Chris was holding tight to her control. It was just another one of Lenora's dramas, the twenty-twenty hindsight she tried to skew into foreknowledge. "There was nothing wrong with the car, Mom. You know that."

Lenora opened her eyes and kept going like she hadn't heard her daughter. "I told you that caving in to his demands and giving it to him, when he'd done nothing to deserve it, was just asking for trouble. Spoiling him, encouraging him in his disobedience, just because it was the easy way. You should have nipped that in the bud, all that backtalk, the drugs, and he'd still be here. Your son would still be alive if you'd been a better parent."

Growing up, Chris had believed she'd had a terrible temper, that she was a naturally angry person. It had contributed to her decision, in her twenties, not to have children. Because she saw herself as someone without control, a woman who wouldn't be able to stop the fury coming out of her mouth when she was crossed, and she didn't want to inflict that on another generation. It wasn't until she'd moved out and was far away from her mother's influence that her calm nature had been able to assert itself.

The way Chris felt now, staring at Lenora, the way her vision shifted like a switch from one camera to another, was how she'd felt her entire adolescence. Burning and shaking with her own unspent rage and hatred, and always impotent to do anything about it. Back then, it was never worth the cost, the endless grudges Lenora could hold. But now, in the clarity of the morning light streaming through the windows of the house she'd lived in with Trey, she realized she didn't give a shit. There was nothing left to lose.

She advanced on the table fast enough to make her mother cringe backward. She slapped her hands down and leaned in, ignoring the flash of pain where her pinky used to be. She got close to Lenora's face and smelled her rancid breath.

"I was a better mother than you ever were, Mom. All the more so because I had nothing but a template of what *not* to do. You don't love me, and you never did, but I've loved Trey from the moment I knew I was carrying him. You're wrong about sacrifice. It's not about saying no to everything, just to teach kids a lesson, put them in their place. And they don't owe us shit for what we give up for them. It travels one direction, Mom, and if Trey ever has kids of his own, I hope he figures that out real quick. I think he will, because of how I raised him. I gave up a lot for Trey—I still do, but the difference is I don't resent it. I don't want anything in return, don't need his eternal gratitude. It's a gift to be his mother, and I'll *never* finish paying off that debt."

She pushed off from the table, no longer shaking, but calm and somehow cleaner, washed free. None of the vitriol she'd planned to spew at her mother had come out of her mouth, and she was glad. What she'd said had been her own truth, and it had let her see clearly what had become muddled over the last few days. She'd meant every word of what she'd said—she didn't expect anything in return for what she gave up for Trey—not even a guarantee of success. Because even if all she bought with her life was a chance for her son, it was worth it.

She looked down at Lenora and for the first time, she felt nothing. Not pity or remorse. Not hatred or resentment. It was her long held and shameful secret, that she would be happier once her mother was gone. Now she didn't have to wait for that, and Chris felt buoyant with the knowledge that she'd never have to see her again.

She turned her back and headed for the stairs. "I'm going up to change clothes. I don't want you to be here when I get back down. Leave your key on the table." She made it almost to the top before her mother found her voice.

"He's dead, Christine."

Chris turned and looked down at Lenora, looking smaller than she ever had. "You think I don't know that?"

Lenora shook her head, frowning. "You said, if he ever has children of his own. He's dead—he can't."

Chris smiled, raised an eyebrow. "No? Oh well, my mistake."

She hadn't planned to take a shower, but once she got upstairs, she wanted one. Probably something symbolic in that, she thought, washing away the burdens of the past. And by the time she stepped out and wrapped a towel around her dripping body, she knew how she would kill herself.

CHAPTER TWENTY

Dan stood vigil at his kitchen window; a vantage he'd gotten used to staring from. He kept an eye on the empty pavement beneath the streetlight, where he'd once seen *something* standing there with Chris in the small hours of the morning, though he didn't know what. Every so often his eyes would stray to Chris's bedroom window, or to the one in the kitchen, waiting for movement. Toots sat at his side, pawing at his leg whenever he stopped scratching beneath her collar.

The strange car was gone, an angry looking old woman having peeled out twenty minutes before, nearly taking out one of the neighbor's mailboxes on her way out. Chris's mother, if he had to guess, and he hoped it meant Chris had given the woman a piece of her mind. He knew this was the last day, though she hadn't said so. He'd felt it when he woke and found her side of the bed empty, and he didn't want these last precious hours tainted.

After another ten minutes he felt like a stalker, so he went to the table to wait for her, his mind the same tangle of indecision it had been since Chris told him she was leaving. He wasn't stupid, though he'd been playing like he was, even to himself. A person didn't "go away" and never come back unless they either offed themselves, or went into witness protection, and he hadn't seen any government agents coming around to whisk his girlfriend away.

Girlfriend. Dan smirked at the word. It didn't seem applicable at their age, the way it had when he was younger. Not because they were too old, it was just that their connection seemed more than that frivolous term implied. He'd admired Chris for years, and had felt, the first time they met, that she was going to be special somehow. He hadn't spent the years since she'd moved in next door alone and pining—he'd ask her out periodically, she'd turn him down, and he'd find someone else for a little while, though she was never far from his thoughts. She was strong and smart and beautiful, and if these had been normal circumstances, he'd have already been shopping for a ring.

They weren't normal circumstances, though, and he supposed he'd known that even that first night she'd finally kissed him. Something had to have happened, changed for her somehow, to open that door she'd kept shut between them. He'd figured it had to do with her son, and over time he'd put together that she had some kind of ritual she did every day. He'd had his suspicions, watching those cuts bloom all over her body, a new one every day, and then when she'd mutilated her leg like that, and amputated her own finger...

His stomach churned with guilt and nausea. He should have called someone at that point, if not before. Her ex-husband, or a doctor, or someone. She couldn't be in her right mind to do something like that, cutting that square of skin out of her own thigh. He wondered how she'd made herself do it, and how she'd brought that blade down on her own hand. She didn't seem irrational, or hysterical, when she wasn't doing those things, but he was no judge. And now he knew there was no excuse for letting her continue on this path. She planned to kill herself. No matter what white lies they told one another, it was the only possible conclusion. He knew he should stop her, even if she hated him for it. That someone contemplating suicide was, by definition, suffering from a mental illness, and as such she needed help. If she succeeded, which she surely would, he'd be as guilty as if he'd pulled the trigger himself. Getting her help was the right thing, and Dan was a man who always did the right thing.

Except that, contrary to his strict Catholic upbringing, Dan didn't believe that suicide was the ultimate sin. There was a time and place for it, though few and far between. He had no problem with it as a method to end suffering—he wouldn't fault someone who took their own life in the midst of a painful terminal illness. And no matter the reason, he didn't believe his God would ever turn his back on someone suffering enough to take that step.

What was the difference, really, between physical pain caused by say, cancer, and the living hell Chris had been in since the day her son was killed?

He'd asked her, years ago now, when Trey was a teenager and she spent every weekend attending early morning baseball games and taking him to practice three nights a week, how she could stand to devote that much time to it when she didn't even like sports. She'd smiled and told him she'd felt the same way, back before she'd become a mother.

"I used to feel sorry for those parents sitting in the bleachers," she'd said, pushing sweaty hair from her forehead, watching her son careen around the yard gathering equipment he'd flung any-where and everywhere. "But after he got here? All I've ever wanted since then is to be where he is. So if he's out in the swel-tering heat playing baseball, then that's the only place I want to be."

Though he still didn't understand it, he knew it was true for her, and the day he'd learned of Trey's death that conversation came to mind. The only place Chris ever wanted to be was gone forever, and Dan had felt a deep foreboding about his neighbor. Two years later, it looked as though those concerns had been merited.

The strange thing was, he didn't believe she was doing it out of despair. She seemed happy these days, more like her old self than he'd seen in ages. He knew that was often the case for people contemplating suicide, that with the decision made, they were happier, more relaxed, but he didn't think that was it, either. Chris didn't want to leave. Which left the only possible conclusion: she was doing it for her son, somehow. He didn't know what good she thought she could do Trey by dying, but then, he hadn't asked.

Little though it appealed to him, he decided, as he sat waiting for her return, that he would have to. He would let Chris be the deciding factor in whether he intervened. If she were planning it out of despair, or if she seemed delusional in her reasoning, he'd have no choice, even if she hated him for it. He wasn't sure what other options there were. He couldn't picture a lucid, reasonable excuse for death, but he wasn't ready to rat her out yet. He told himself he had time. They both did.

CHAPTER TWENTY-ONE

Funny how those last hours seemed both rushed and drawn out. How often Dan would check the time, feeling his stomach drop when he saw how much had slipped away. Yet the love they made was slow and sweet, and the words they shared were unrushed. He tried and failed several times to bring it up, to ask the question he most needed an answer to. When he finally did, she didn't answer him at first, but she didn't seem angry, either.

She turned to lie on her side, the curve of her bare hips lit by a soft lamp. It was a beautiful landscape he never got enough of. "What did you see, the night you were in your kitchen while I was out there?"

His face reddened and she smiled. "It's not like you were spying on me. If you left every night at the same time with no explanation, I'd have probably been going through your phone to see who you were meeting."

He moved closer and ran his fingertips along her side, stopping to cup one heavy breast. "I don't know what I saw.

Something was out there with you, or someone. It was weird—I could see you plain as day, under the light, but the other..." He frowned, ran his hand around to her back and pulled her closer, her nipples hard against his bare chest. "It was darker, somehow. Couldn't make much out, 'specially when I tried looking straight at it."

She pulled away to look at him. "You saw him, though?" Her body was tense under his hands, and he saw in her eyes how much she needed this.

It was now or never. He could tell her he hadn't seen a person, ease her toward the idea of getting some help. Dash her dreams and if she didn't come around, step in against her will. But he couldn't do that to her and lying didn't come easy.

"I guess I did," he answered, and she melted against him. A minute later her shoulders were shaking, and he felt warm tears against his skin.

"I missed him so goddamn much," she said, her voice half muffled. "I never knew anything could hurt that bad, the wanting. The giant fucking hole he left in my life. I couldn't breathe. I still can't if I think about it too hard. And then one night he came back to me."

She told him all of it. Every step along her path to the decision she'd finally come to, and though it hurt his very soul to hear it, he could see it, exactly how she'd come to where she was now. It was possible she was crazy, that she'd imagined the whole thing, just as she had her continued conversations with Trey for the past year. But that was the thing—she knew the difference between the two. She even told him of her uncertainty on what method to use to end her own life.

"But I think I know now. I'm not a hundred percent sure—I don't think there's any way I can be."

He sat up, pulled her up with him so she rested against his chest and he didn't have to hold that bright, hard gaze. "So you're not sure this is going to work?"

She laughed. "How the hell could I be? This isn't a fantasy novel, or a movie where I cast a specific spell and it brings my son back to life. The whole thing could be bullshit."

He didn't know whether her lucidity made it better or worse. "Then how..." he stopped, but she waited him out. "How do you know it's worth it, then? If there's a chance the whole thing is just...a delusion, or something."

She leaned back into him. "It's not a delusion," she said in a low, dreamy voice. "You seeing him proves that. My son has been visiting me, and my best information suggests this is the way to help him."

He thought again about that dark figure, how hard it had been to see. How it didn't look a damn thing like Trey. "And you're sure...you're certain it's him? That it's Trey out there, and not something else?"

Her body was tense against him, her nails dug lightly into his thighs, then relaxed. "I'm sure. I know my own son."

He knew then that she was lying, that she'd experienced her own doubt. Just as he knew she would never admit it, so he let that part go, and tried another tack. "Even so, Chris, you don't know it'll work. It could be for nothing, and it's a hell of a sacrifice."

She was quiet for a long time, and hope made his stomach turn. Maybe she would walk away from it. Maybe all she'd needed was someone to give her a reason not to take this step.

"It took more than three years to get pregnant with Trey. Did I ever tell you that?"

He looked down at the top of her head, her chestnut hair threaded with silver and glowing in the lamplight. "No, I don't believe you did."

"If you've never wanted kids, never tried to have them, you may not be able to understand what that's like. To watch everyone else on the planet get pregnant at the drop of a hat. To try, and fail, no matter what you do. I told myself when we started, Beau and I, that we were casually trying. That if it happened, or if it didn't, I'd be okay." She laughed. "I had no idea what I was getting into."

She sat up and scooted away so she could face him, pulling the sheet up around her breasts. "Those three years damn near broke me. My life got whittled down to something so narrow I didn't even recognize it. When we finally started getting treatment, it got even worse. Procedures that always hurt like hell. Hormones that drove me crazy, on top of depression I could barely claw my way out of. In the end, none of it had worked, and all we had left was in vitro. I'd never wanted to do that. It's expensive, and invasive, and frankly terrifying."

She met his eyes and smiled. "There were no guarantees then, either. That was the shittiest part. Every step I took down that path sunk me deeper. Made my depression worse, made it harder for me to even see who I used to be. And I never had anything to show for it—no baby, no positive pregnancy test. No answers, either, and staring down the barrel of that process, I knew it would be the deepest hole I'd dug yet. It scared the shit out of me, Dan.

"I thought about walking away. Trying to figure out how to be okay with not being a mother." She took a deep breath. "But I didn't. I took the plunge, and it failed the first time, and I thought oh fuck, what have I done. Because I was right—it was worse than ever, and I didn't think I'd ever recover. But the second time..." Her eyes unfocused and the sweetest smile he'd ever seen curved her lips. "The rest is history. I thought of that a lot, later on. How close I came to walking away, and how glad I was I took that leap of faith."

She scooted close and put a hand to his cheek. "And that's how this feels. Like I'm back there, staring at a dark path and I don't know where it leads. It may lead nowhere. It may lead somewhere worse than here—a lot worse. But it's the only way forward, and I know I'll always regret it, if I don't take that step."

He couldn't answer, but she didn't seem to expect him to. She kissed him, and pulled the sheet from between them, climbing on top of him for what he knew was the last time. When they were finished, she rested on his chest, and though he would have sworn there was no way he could fall asleep knowing how short her time was, he was out before he knew it.

He woke in the deepest, darkest part of the night, and it took a minute for him to realize she was still with him. She'd rolled to the side, no longer touching him, but her chest rose and fell, and he could feel her warmth from across the mattress. He groped for his cell phone and checked the time—an hour. That was all they had left.

He sat on the edge of the bed and thought, his mind in as much turmoil as it had ever been. She knew what she was doing, he had no doubt of that. She was making a measured, considered decision, with full knowledge that it might be in vain. She was an adult, and it was her choice to make, but in the end, he knew he couldn't let her go through with it.

The decision brought him relief, but also a wave of guilt and grief. He pushed off from the side of the bed and found his way in the dark, bent on doing what was right, even when it felt so wrong.

CHAPTER TWENTY-TWO

C hris was alone in Dan's bed when she woke, but with the feeling that she'd only just missed him. She couldn't see a clock and didn't know where her cell phone was, but she was calm, knowing she'd woken in time. She stood and dressed in the dark, then padded in silence to the kitchen, stopping on the threshold.

Dan stood over the sink, Toots at his side. He was shirtless and she could tell he was crying from the way his shoulders were shaking. There was a muffled *plink* as several somethings landed in the sink. Chris couldn't place the sound, didn't know what he could be doing until she saw the gun. Her gun, the 9mm semi-auto she'd been taking with her to the cross. He was emptying the magazine bullet by bullet. The slide was back, and she could see the one in the chamber had already been popped.

She sighed and he turned, dropping the empty gun on the counter.

"I'm sorry, Chris," he said in a hoarse whisper, and she knew how wrong she'd been to bring him into this, to put him through this turmoil. It hadn't been fair to him, and she felt like a shit.

"I'm so sorry, but I can't let you do it. I thought I could, because no matter how it sounds, I know you're not crazy. I just can't let you make the trade, honey."

"Shhh." She went to him and wrapped her arms around him, let him cry on her shoulder.

"If I knew for sure it would work like you say, I think I'd be able to step back. But I'm afraid, Chris, and I can't do it. I should never have said I would. And I'm sorry if you hate me, I'll understand, but I have to stop you, okay? I have to keep you here."

"Okay, Dan. It's okay, and I don't hate you. You're not going to have to stop me, okay? It's not fair of me to put that on you, so I'm sorry. Let's forget it."

He pulled back and held her shoulders, his gaze searching hers. "You're not gonna do it?"

She gave a tired smile. "Not tonight, at least, okay? It's too late anyway. We can talk about it tomorrow, but I think maybe you're right. I think I might have had this whole thing wrong. Come back to bed, will you?"

She could tell he wanted to believe her, but he didn't quite. She figured he planned to stay awake and keep her from changing her mind, but she knew there wasn't much she could do about it at this point, and she felt a calm certainty that things were working out as they were meant to. So she coaxed him back to bed, and she guessed from the glance he cast to her purse that he'd already done something with her car keys.

No matter. It was out of her hands now, and there was peace in that.

*

Dan had in fact meant to stay awake. He'd been terrified, and in such emotional upheaval, he would have bet anything against his being able to close his eyes again that night. But somehow, maybe it was just the relief of it, the cautious happiness that maybe they were coming out the other side of this thing. Whatever was at work that night, he drifted out of consciousness not long after returning to bed. He felt heavy, his mind foggy, and he tried to remind himself to tell her something that felt urgent. It was about what he'd seen that night under the streetlight. It was true, what he'd said, about it being dark and hard to make out, but it was more than that. Whatever was out there had been *wrong*, and he couldn't let her follow it. His conviction had grown stronger the more he'd thought about it, tried to focus his memory on what it might have been. And as he'd stood over the sink, emptying the bullets from the gun he was sure she'd meant to use on herself, he'd looked up and seen it again. Something dark, something wrong, waiting under that streetlight. Waiting and watching Dan. As he fought to struggle back to the surface of consciousness, he didn't understand why he hadn't mentioned it. He told himself it didn't matter, that he would have time to convince her, and then he was gone, buried in a suffocating, heavy blackness that allowed no breath, and no doubt.

CHAPTER TWENTY-THREE

In the end she hadn't needed the gun. Hadn't needed her car, either. The walk should have seemed long and frigid in the November frost, but she barely remembered it, and it seemed like no time at all before she was there.

She had no concept of what time it was. The walk should have taken at least an hour, maybe more, but the night was still in its deepest dark. There were no cars on the highway above, no stars, no streetlights. She couldn't remember if that was right or not— had there been light before? There must have been, or else how could she have seen? But then she'd always come at dusk, not full night, so it was hard to tell.

She made her way down the steep grade by memory and instinct, with the feeling of being guided by someone just out of sight. It felt as though a hand were extended to her in the darkness, just out of reach. Trey's hand, she hoped, though she hadn't yet seen him. Her feet slipped on the frost-covered ground and she slid the last few feet on her ass, only then realizing she was barefoot.

She was alone in the hollow. She looked around, trying to make out shapes in the black, but the only thing she could see clearly was the cross, gleaming in the center of the darkness. She stepped toward it, still looking around for him. For Trey. She'd thought she'd get to see him one last time, maybe even hold his hand as her life ebbed away, but she was utterly alone in the place she would die.

Thinking, in a hazy, muddled way, of Dan, and the pain she'd caused him, she realized it was only right that she do this alone. Though it might comfort her to have Trey's company, it would be agony to him, and she wanted him to start fresh, with a clear conscience. She thought of his life, opening again like a bright highway, his future brimming with possibilities. She pictured him driving his Camaro into the promise of a new morning, and she smiled even as tears coursed down her cheeks.

The shovel was waiting for her, propped behind the cross where she hadn't been able to see it before, and it reassured her that she was on the right track. The blade bit into the frozen ground and she felt it jar her arms all the way back to her shoulders. The place where her pinky used to be was a white-hot flame of agony, but she tightened her grip and kept digging. For now, she would just dig, so she didn't have to think about what came next.

The wind was still as she worked, the leaves motionless and silent in their branches. And yet, what was that noise like a moan? It was the same noise she'd heard the night she'd amputated her finger. It drifted in and out of her awareness, but much of the time it was muffled by the thick fog she existed in. She felt little, heard little, was a mindless automaton bent on a single task. Dig.

When she was finished, she threw the shovel aside and looked down, finally facing her fear. It was a grave she'd dug; her own. She should have known, the willing enactment of her greatest fear, the nightmare that had plagued her for years—it was the only right answer. Sacrifice was about loss. It was about giving up things you loved, like Dan, and Beau, and the girls, and Penny Lane. It was about doing the things that were hardest, that scared you the most. Motherhood had made her face all her fears, let go of her phobias and the things that bugged her, like snot and puke and having anything touching her collar bone. Kids trample all over those little rules and preferences in no time, and they put you in the most terrifying, godawful positions. Being Trey's mother had been the scariest, most stressful, exhausting, wonderful, and perfect thing she'd ever done. An answer to a thousand prayers, and certainly worth this.

She stared down into the black ground. She didn't know how deep she'd dug, but she couldn't see the bottom or the sides now. For all she knew it could lead straight to hell. The crossroads demon was on her mind and she wondered if she had, in fact, summoned something that first night she bled into the ground here.

She closed her eyes. It didn't matter. Her life, her happiness, her immortal soul—all of it was forfeit for him. She stepped into the grave with her eyes still closed, felt her stomach drop as her feet met nothing below and she tumbled in a short free fall. Then she was down, in the cold ground, swallowed by the dirt as she'd so often dreamed. Her heart worked overtime and her airway closed in panic, but she clutched the ground and waited. She'd made her choice, and she'd be damned if she took it back now.

The dirt began to rain in from above, a shovelful at a time. She opened her eyes, wondering if she'd be able to see him, but her vision was as black as if she'd already died. So she closed her eyes again and lay still while soil pattered over her body, covering her eyes, her closed mouth, and finally her nose.

The wind moaned louder than ever as every trace of Chris was covered. Its cries shook the tree where her son had died, its fury warmed the air. As she breathed her last, she'd have been able to hear it call to her once more, a deep and anguished

Mooooommmmmm! No!

But she couldn't; her ears were packed with dirt, and Chris died without hearing her son's call.

CHAPTER TWENTY-FOUR

"I don't get it," said the man with the cigarette, standing over the open hole, staring down. "How the fuck does anybody bury themselves alive as a means to take their own life?"

His partner looked down from across the grave, trying to keep upwind of the smoke. She heard a clang and watched as the EMTs tried to negotiate the stretcher up the hillside, cringing inside. She hated thinking of that poor woman's body tumbling back down into this pit.

She went back to taking photographs of the scene, like she was supposed to. "I don't know, Mike. I heard her son died a couple years ago; that kind of loss could do it to ya."

Mike shook his head. "That's not what I mean, Tara. We've seen suicides, plenty of 'em. I just don't get the mechanics of it. I mean, how did she get all the dirt in there on top of her? I don't understand how anybody's looking at this as a suicide in the first place. Seems pretty clear to me, there had to be foul play."

Tara hunched a shoulder. "I think right now, it's on account of the note she left, and the self-mutilation. The chick was pretty fucked up, sounds like. I feel bad for her boyfriend." She indicated the man with the Tom Selleck mustache who stood at the top, waiting for the remains of his girlfriend to make it to level ground. "Pretty shitty thing to do to someone who cares about you."

Mike grunted. "You ask me, they oughtta be lookin' real hard at that dude. He had to've known something, don't you think? Either him, or that ex-husband. You remember I said that, Tara. We're gonna find out this wasn't no suicide. *Ow, fuck!*"

Tara nearly dropped her camera, her partner having dropped to one knee, clutching his face. "Mike? You okay? What the fuck happened?"

He moved his hand and a trickle of blood ran from his eyebrow. "Damn, that could've taken my eye out. Where the fuck'd it come from?"

Tara knelt to pick up the box, small and wooden, the carved design filled in with dirt. She pried open the lid, then pulled back. "Oh gross, there's fucking *teeth* in here." She looked closer. "And hair, looks like." She looked up. "This lady into voodoo or something?"

Mike stood, frowning, and peered into the box. "No. This looks more like a memory box, for keepsakes. April has one each for the boys—she's got some of their baby teeth, you know, from the tooth fairy. And hair from their first cuts."

Tara raised an eyebrow and handed him the box. "That's fucking morbid, Mike."

"It's a mom thing," he said with a shrug. He took the box, closed it with care and looked up, scanning for where the relic might have come from. It looked like it had been buried, maybe even unearthed by the vic when she'd been digging that grave. But it had come from above, must have, unless someone had chucked it at him.

He frowned, seeing movement way up, in one of the big tree's crotches. Something glinted, and he could make out a wad of something up there, almost looked like a bird's nest. Ignoring Tara's protests, he stripped off his coat and set to climbing. Not for nothing had he raised two boys to adolescence in the country.

He shimmied up, the old oak's branches providing plenty of hand and foot holds. Almost to his goal, he looked down and saw his partner standing with her hands on her hips, yelling something he couldn't hear. He waved at her, turned to make the last part of the climb, and pulled himself eye level with the clump that had caught his eye.

"Oh, Jesus," he said, gagging. It wasn't the shirt that bothered him, or the gleaming diamond ring wedged tight to the trunk. It was the severed finger, gray and dirty, lying on top of a jagged cut square of what might be flesh. It was all gathered close together, laid out like someone's treasures. How did it all get up here?

He could hear the faint sound of Tara shouting below, but he still couldn't make out what she was saying. Then the wind picked up, the branches swaying, leaves rustling, and a strange moaning started. Strange most of all because of how close it was, almost right on top of him. He felt the cold touch at the same time he looked up to see the dark-eyed shadow crouching over him.

Mike had a minute to take in the face, the mournful, tear-filled eyes, the neck canted at a wrong angle, a mashed in skull and hair sticky and matted with blood. The moan rose again, and Mike screamed, lurched away, and let go. He crashed through branches on his way down, no time to think of the injuries he was collecting as he went. As he lay on the ground after impact, oblivious to the screams of his partner and the frenzied movements of the medics, he knew what he had heard. He wished he knew who that dead thing's mother was, so he could bring her to it, because he'd never heard such anguish before. He wasn't likely to again, he thought, as darkness edged out his vision.

Acknowledgements

I am immensely lucky to have so many people to be grateful to, even more so than the first time around. Writing is a strange and sometimes solitary journey, but it's one we accomplish not so much on an isolated path, but one on which our companions are just out of sight, walking with us, and ready to meet at the next crossroads. My fellow travelers include, in no particular order:

Rich Duncan and Shane Douglas Keene, my brothers in horror, who support me every day. I would never have tried my hand at shorter fiction, were it not for them, and they're quick to offer an insightful beta read, many words of encouragement, and to calm down my occasional freak outs. They were some of the first readers of this novella, and without them it wouldn't be here. They also provide endless laughs when we all need it most. Love you guys, ya goints.

My horror girls, Jessica Clark and Stephanie Woolery, for always being excited for me, and also for movie marathons, ren faire adventures, and giggly drink fests. I have no idea what we laugh about most of the time, but it's healing, and it's necessary. Wouldn't want to do this thing without you, ladies. A short beer on me, next time we go.

A big thank you to Daron Kappauff and Kevin Whitten, otherwise known as Well Read Beard. They gave graciously of their time to lay early eyes on this manuscript, and gave invaluable insight that made it a better story. These are two of the coolest dudes I've met since venturing into the strange land of Twitter, and I'm glad to call y'all friends.

Speaking of the Twittersphere, I never, in all my weird girl introverted life, dreamt I would come to love an online home as much as I do our horror family. The folks I have met, from reviewers, to writers, to geeky folks whose virtual paths have serendipitously crossed mine, have made my life richer. If I tried to name you all, I'd inevitably fail, and it would keep me up at night, so suffice it to say if you're one of my Tweeps, this bourbon's for you. Thank you for being there.

On the subject of reviewers, a huge thank you to this eclectic and giving group of folks. Without your reviews, there'd still be tumbleweeds rolling through Goodreads, so I thank you from the bottom of my heart. Whether you love my work, hate it, or are left with meh, you gave of your time, and for that I'm grateful. There are again far too many to name, but special thanks to Sian Plummer, Lilyn George, and the entire Sci Fi & Scary team, to Patrick McDonough, Elle Turpitt, Brennan LeFaro and Ellen Avigliano of Deadhead Reviews, John Lynch, Matt Redmon, Sadie Hartmann, Ashley Saywers, and the whole Night Worms crew, as well as the Ladies of Horror Fiction team, and Horror Aficionados. The majority of reviewers do so for no compensation, and they're invaluable to the profession. Treat them well and buy them drinks.

To my fellow horror authors, so many of whom have given of their time to help advise, read, or lift up a newbie. You are my circle, my inspiration, and my friends. Horror family for life. Special thanks to Jonathan Janz for giving so generously of his time to offer advice, and to Josh Malerman, for making time for an early read and words of encouragement.

To Karmen Wells, for eagle eyed and compassionate editing. Thank you for making this a better book.

To Cody Luff, the author of the horror novel *Ration*, for graciously allowing me to reference it in this manuscript. It's a fantastic book and you should go read it right now.

To Samantha Kolesnik, who has been an author's dream to work with. I'm lucky you added running a press to your list of accomplishments, and I can't wait to read everything Off Limits Press puts out.

To the teachers that shoulder a thankless task everyday. We've been lucky to have had some of the most amazing ones over the last couple of years, and I could not do what I do without knowing you're doing what you do.

To my mother, Lynn Hightower, for encouraging my writing from a young age, and for proving it can be done, by living it everyday.

To Rachel Ballard and Alan Hightower, for being family I'd choose myself. Glad the genetic lottery put us all together, you incredibly fabulous people, you. To Wes Ballard and Katie Stephens, who were just siblings waiting to happen. To Isaac and Everett, two amazing nephews I'm glad to call mine.

To Julia Ritchie, for author photos I love, though not as much as I love you. To Allison Saxton, for a beautiful website, advice and support, as well as that nudge into social media I so clearly needed. Also for being a generally awesome friend. To Young Eun Park, for reading, being my friend, letting me keep you after you left, and for the best memes ever.

To my job, for keeping it interesting, and also being the kind of place that gives a girl head space to write. Y'all celebrate every milestone with me, and your support means the world. Thanks for letting me make a home here.

To Arthur Wells, who will always be my oldest kiddo. You're the best big brother, and a son to be proud of. Let's drink bourbon together soon.

To David, for being my partner in everything. After fifteen years you still make me laugh, and if that's not the key to a good marriage, I don't know what is. Unless it's blueberry pancakes, and you have that covered, too.

And to Sebastian. Will I ever stop getting teary eyed when I think of the long road it took to meet you? Who knows. We're getting better on the time to write thing, but no matter what, it's always for you, Tiny Buddy.

Laurel Hightower grew up in Kentucky, attending college in California and Tennessee before returning home to horse country, where she lives with her husband, son, and two rescue animals. She works as a paralegal in a mid-size firm, wrangling litigators by day and writing at night. A bourbon and beer girl, she's a fan of horror movies and true-life ghost stories. Her debut novel, *Whispers in the Dark*, was published in 2018.

9 780578 723563